Riding with the James Gang

a Luke and Jenny Adventure

RIDING WITH THE JAMES GANG

a Luke and Jenny Adventure

Gayle Martin

FIVE STAR LEGENDS

Five Star Publications, Inc.
P. O. Box 6698
Chandler, AZ 85246 U.S.A.
480-940-8182 • Toll Free 1-866-471-0777

Publisher's Cataloging-In-Publication Data
(Prepared by The Donohue Group, Inc.)

Martin, Gayle, 1956-
   Riding with the James gang / by Gayle Martin.

   p. ; cm.

   Summary: As their summer vacation draws to a close, Luke and Jenny have camped out on their great-grandmother's back porch. But their sweet dreams are interrupted when Kate, the ghost of a young farm girl, takes them back in time and they discover the life and times of the James-Younger gang.
   Includes biogeographical references.
   "A Luke and Jenny adventure."
   Interest age level: 009-012.
   ISBN: 978-1-58985-164-1

1. Outlaws--West (U.S.)--History--19th century--Juvenile fiction. 2. West
(U.S.)--History--1860-1890--Juvenile fiction. 3. Time travel--
Juvenile
fiction. 4. Ghosts--Juvenile fiction. 5. Outlaws--West (U.S.)--
History--19th
century--Fiction. 6. West (U.S.)--History--1860-1890--Fiction. 7.
Time travel--Fiction. 8. Ghosts--Fiction. I. Title.

PZ7.M362 Ri 2010
[Fic]

EDITOR: Sachiyo Ragsdale
TYPESETTING: Arizona Living History Press, LLC
ILLUSTRATOR: Wes Lowe
COVER DESIGN: Arizona Living History Press, LLC

To Sam, who first introduced me to the world of living history, and to Anne, who first encouraged me to become an author. I would not be where I am today if not for you.

Table of Contents

Chapter One
Great Grandma Katie 1

Chapter Two
A Ghost in the Cornfield 7

Chapter Three
Quantrill's Raiders 14

Chapter Four
Jesse Joins the Militia 22

Chapter Five
Quantrill's Ghost 28

Chapter Six
Buck and Dingus 35

Chapter Seven
The Liberty Bank Robbery 40

Chapter Eight
The Russellville Bank Robbery 44

Chapter Nine
Jesse James Gets a Price on His Head 49

Chapter Ten
A Raid on the James Farm 53

Chapter Eleven
The Kansas City Fair 57

Chapter Twelve
The James-Younger Gang Robs a Train 60

Chapter Thirteen
The Death of John Younger 66

Chapter Fourteen
Jesse James Takes a Bride 74

Chapter Fifteen
The Pinkerton Raid 77

Chapter Sixteen
Bob Younger Backs a Bad Idea 81

Chapter Seventeen
The Rocky Cut Train Robbery 86

Chapter Eighteen
The Northfield, Minnesota, Bank Robbery 90

Chapter Nineteen
A Painful Journey Begins 96

Chapter Twenty
The Younger Brothers' Final Shoot-out 101

Chapter Twenty-One
Hard Times for Jesse James 108

Chapter Twenty-Two
The Glendale Train Robbery 112

Chapter Twenty-Three
Frank Gets Back in the Game 116

Chapter Twenty-Four
No Turning Back 119

Chapter Twenty-Five
The Dirty Little Coward Who Shot Mr. Howard 124

Chapter Twenty-Six
Breakfast at Great Grandma's House 131

Chapter One
Great Grandma Katie

Luke reached across the picnic table for another piece of fried chicken.

"Hold it right there, young man!" scolded his mother. "That's bad manners. You ask someone to pass the chicken to you. Then you may take another piece."

"Sorry, Mom," said Luke as he waited for the platter of chicken to be passed his way. When he picked up a drumstick his sister Jenny chided: "Gee, Luke, isn't that your fourth piece?"

She flipped her long blonde ponytail back as she spoke.

"Are you going for a world's record or something?"

"Wouldn't talk, smarty pants! You've already eaten five ears of corn!"

Before their mother could break up their argument Luke and Jenny started giggling at one another. The white-haired elderly woman seated at the head of the table reached over to tap her on the arm.

"Now, Ellen, it's been such a wonderful day, and I've been so happy to finally meet my great grandchildren. How old are they again?"

"Luke is eight, and Jenny is ten."

"My goodness. It seems like just yesterday they were born. They grow up so fast, don't you know. Let them enjoy their picnic."

It had been a fine day indeed. Luke and Jenny had come with their mother to meet their great grandmother, Katie, who lived on a farm in Missouri. They had never been on a real farm before. It was certainly different from their home in Phoenix. There was a rustic old barn, and Luke had been fascinated by the grain silo. He imagined it to be the tower of an old medieval castle. The farm made the perfect backdrop for a big family backyard picnic. The rolling hills and lush fields of green seemed to go on forever, making their great grandmother's "back yard" the biggest one they'd ever seen.

Today's picnic would mark the end of their summer vacation. The following morning they would begin their journey home. And while it wasn't the vacation they had planned, they were both sad to see it come to an end.

Their parents had planned to take them to Disneyland. But then Luke and Jenny's father, who was in the Army Reserve, had been sent to Iraq. He would be gone for at least a year. And while it was hard on all of them, it had been especially rough on Luke. He felt as if he had lost his very best friend. Their mother had tried to make it up to them the best she could. Instead of Disneyland she decided they would take a trip to Dallas to visit their grandparents. Along the way she planned a few side trips so it would seem more like a real vacation.

Their first stop was Tombstone, Arizona, where Wyatt Earp and his brothers had once lived. A couple days later they stopped in Lincoln, New Mexico, and followed the footsteps of Billy the Kid.

Once they arrived in Texas they had a wonderful visit with their grandparents. They even went to Six Flags Over Texas, a nearby amusement park where Luke and his grandfather rode one of the roller coasters six times in a row. It may not have been Disneyland, but it was certainly a lot of fun. And while it didn't quite make up for their father's absence, both Luke and Jenny enjoyed spending time with their grandparents. When the time came for them to leave, they both felt sad. They hoped to be able to come back and see their grandparents more often.

While they were in Dallas their mother decided they would drive to Missouri so she could visit her grandmother. She explained that her grandmother was now in her nineties and she wanted to see her for what would probably be the last time. Luke and Jenny were glad she did. They both enjoyed meeting their great grandmother and they loved visiting a real farm.

"So how old is your farmhouse again, Great Grandma?" asked Luke as he bit into his piece of chicken.

"Well, let's see... As I recall, the original part of the house was built back in 1919, shortly after the end of World War I. It was built to replace the house your great grandfather's folks had built after the Civil War. By the time I came here as a young bride in 1934, more rooms had been added. We added on another room the following year, when your great uncle Carl was born. I had five other children after that; your great aunts Leona, Grace and Ellen, whom your mother was named after. We built the second-story in the 1940s, after your great aunt Ellen was born."

"I didn't know I had such a big family," said Jenny. "So then Grandmother Angela in Dallas..."

"Is my youngest daughter," said Great Grandmother Katie. "Then after her came your great uncle Julian. He was the baby of the family. He was killed in Vietnam in 1967."

Great Grandmother Katie looked sad for a moment. Then she spoke to Luke and Jenny's mother.

"You know, it's funny. I had a dream about Julian the other night and it all seemed so real that it didn't even feel like a dream at all. I saw him standing at the foot of my bed, clear as day, and he was talking to me about you, Ellen. He said to tell you that he was watching out for Jason in Iraq and to let you know he'd be coming home safely."

"Now, Grandma, that's really sweet, but it was only a dream."

Great Grandmother Katie shrugged her shoulders and looked at Luke and Jenny.

"That's the way your mother has always been. She's the skeptic in this family. If she can't see it or hear it or touch it then she doesn't believe in it."

"So our family must really go back a long way here," said Jenny, wanting to change the subject.

"Yes indeed," replied Uncle Carl, who sat across the table from her. "Our family started farming this land before the Civil War, but times have changed. Your Aunt Vickie and I are the last ones here. Everyone else scattered across the country and took regular jobs." He sighed. "You know, I can't say I really blame 'em. Farming is hard and dangerous work. And it's risky too. If your crops fail, you could lose everything."

"And that's why we've leased out our land to a corporation," added Aunt Vickie as she patted her husband's arm. "They're working the land now. So don't let your uncle fool you. Nowadays he's just a weekend farmer."

"Still, this place must have a lot of history," said Ellen. "I remember when I used to visit here as a little girl and you two would tell me stories about Frank and Jesse James."

Luke suddenly perked up.

"Frank and Jesse James? Did they live around here?"

"They certainly did, young man," said Great Grandmother Katie. "Their farm was up in Kearney—not too far from here. And now it's a museum."

She looked at her granddaughter.

"You know, Ellen, since you've been taking them to all those historic places, you might want to think about taking them to see the James Farm before you head back to Phoenix."

"Can we go, Mom? Can we? Please," begged Luke.

His mother laughed and nodded her head. Her short

curly blonde hair gleamed in the late afternoon sunlight. She looked at her aunt and uncle.

"I can't believe this is the same kid I had to practically drag out of the car when we got to Tombstone. Must have been all the stories the locals told them while we were there. They all claimed the town was haunted. You know me. I had to explain to them that there's no such thing as ghosts."

As they listened to their mother talk Luke and Jenny couldn't help but recall their Tombstone adventure. While they were there they met one of the town ghosts, although he preferred to be called a spirit person. He called himself the Swamper, and he took Luke and Jenny back in time where they found themselves face to face with the Earp brothers and Doc Holliday.

"Then they'll probably like the James Farm," added Aunt Vickie. "I don't know if it's haunted or not, but the James brothers were every bit as notorious as Billy the Kid."

She stopped and thought for a moment.

"I wonder if they ever met."

"No, they never did," said Luke.

Jenny kicked her brother under the table.

"How would you know?" she asked.

"I looked up Billy the Kid on the Internet while we were in Dallas," he replied.

Jenny let out a little sigh of relief. Since their mother had made it clear that there were no such things as ghosts it would have been hard to explain that while they were in Lincoln they met the ghost of Paul. Paul had been a buffalo soldier stationed at Fort Stanton, near the town of Lincoln, more than a century ago. And like the Swamper, he too had taken Luke and Jenny on a journey back in time where they observed firsthand the life and times of Billy the Kid.

"Well, I guess it's time to get the ice cream," said Uncle Carl as he stood up from the picnic table. "Looks like it's going to be getting dark pretty soon."

"Luke, Jenny, you two go and help your aunt clear the table," said their mother. "Before we have dessert I want to spend some quality time with my grandmother."

A short time later, while they were all enjoying their ice cream, Luke and Jenny gazed out across the cornfields. As they watched the sky turn pink and orange with the setting sun they tried to imagine what it would have been like when Frank and Jesse James lived nearby.

Chapter Two

A Ghost in the Cornfield

This was to be their last night at Great Grandmother Katie's house. Luke and Jenny wanted to do something special. They wanted to camp out in the barn. Their uncle Carl had told them stories about all the animals he and his sisters and baby brother had raised on their farm when they were youngsters. Back then there had been horses and ponies, dairy cows, pigs and chickens. But those days were long gone. The only animals left on the farm now were Rufus, Aunt Vickie's sheepdog, and a few outdoor cats. The barn was now being used for storing some of the large pieces of equipment belonging to the company leasing the farm, and the only animals living in it were field mice. Their mother had made it quite clear that she thought it was much too dangerous for them to sleep out in the barn. Luke and Jenny were disappointed, but when Great Grandmother Katie suggested they could camp out on the screened-in back porch instead their mother agreed.

As she settled into her sleeping bag, Jenny reached into her backpack for her journal and began writing. Luke, as usual, was playing with his Game Boy as he settled into his sleeping bag. They could hear the grown-ups inside the house playing cards. It was a pleasant ending to a pleasant day.

"Jenny, can I ask you a question?"

"Sure, Luke, what is it?"

"How come you like to write in your journal?"

"I just like to write about stuff." She paused for a moment. "You know, I've been thinking. I think I'd like to be a reporter when I grow up. I'd like to work for one of those travel magazines. Then I can travel all over the world and write about all the things I see."

"Have you been writing anything in your journal about what happened to us in Tombstone and in Lincoln? When we met the Swamper and Paul and when they took us back in time?"

"No, Luke, I haven't."

"How come?"

Jenny thought carefully before she answered her brother's question.

"Because we have to be careful, Luke. It's like Paul told us. We have a gift. We can see things that most people can't."

She paused for a moment and looked at her brother.

"Why all the questions?"

"Because something's been bothering me."

"What?"

"I feel like we're being secretive by not telling Mom about it."

"I know what you mean, Luke. But even if we tried to tell her about it she'd never believe us. She'd probably say we were making it all up."

"Yeah! And then maybe she'd ground us. And I don't think it's right that we should get grounded when we haven't done anything wrong."

"I know. I've been thinking about that too. And if we really were doing something wrong then yes, we'd also be in the wrong for keeping it from her."

"But if we did tell her, she might think we're nutty, like Aunt Tina."

Aunt Tina was their father's younger sister. She was an astrologer and the assistant manager of a new age bookstore in Tucson. Aunt Tina had always been kind to Luke and Jenny, and they were fond of her too. But they also knew their mother didn't approve of her. And while she knew it would be wrong to discourage her children from having a good relationship with their aunt, she had told them that she thought Aunt Tina's beliefs were nonsense.

"You know, Luke, while we were in Dallas, I had an instant messenger chat with Aunt Tina about it."

"Really? What did she say? Did she believe you?"

"Of course she believed me. She's a psychic, you know. She says sometimes she sees spirit people too. But she also warned me that we should be discreet about it. Otherwise people might think we're crazy."

"That's messed up," said Luke. "People shouldn't think you're crazy just because you can do things they can't."

"I know. But that's what Aunt Tina said. She says there are a lot of skeptics out there, just like Mom. Only she says that some of them can be very, very mean just because you happen to believe in things that they don't. But she also said we can talk to her about it anytime we want to."

"That's good."

Luke went back to his Game Boy while Jenny went back to writing in her journal. A few minutes later their uncle Carl came out on the porch.

"Okay, you guys, it's time for lights out."

Both Luke and Jenny groaned in protest, but their great uncle reminded them they had a big day ahead of them tomorrow. Their mother was going to take them to the James Farm before they started home.

"Are you two going to be warm enough?" he asked. "Sometimes it can get pretty cool out here at night."

"We're fine," answered Jenny. "We're both sleeping in our sweats, and Aunt Vickie brought us some extra blankets just in case we need them."

"Then it looks like you guys are okay. Have a good night."

He turned off the light and told them their mother would be coming out in a little while to check on them. As they listened to him going back into the house their eyes adjusted to the darkness. They noticed the full moon lighting the night sky.

"Jenny!"

"What is it now, Luke?"

"I thought I saw someone walking around in the cornfield."

Jenny rolled over on her stomach and propped her head on her elbows. She stared into the cornfield.

"See that?"

"Shhh! Keep your voice down," she whispered back at her brother. "Do you want the whole world to hear you?"

She studied the cornfield again.

"You're right, Luke. There's something moving around in the cornfield. It's probably Rufus."

"I think Rufus is in the house with the grown-ups," replied Luke.

He paused and thought it over for a minute.

"I guess it must be one of the cats."

"Whatever, Luke. I'm tired. I want to go to sleep."

Luke settled back in his sleeping bag. Moments later he and Jenny began to doze off.

* * *

THUD!

Luke and Jenny suddenly woke up after hearing a loud banging noise. They both sat up and looked around.

"Jenny," whispered Luke, "did Mom just come in here

to check on us?"

They listened closely for a few moments. Then they heard the sound of the grandfather clock chiming inside the house. It struck three times. They realized the grown-ups would all be in bed by now.

"No, it definitely wasn't Mom," she whispered back, not wanting her little brother to worry. "Uncle Carl says there's a lot of raccoons around here. I'll bet that's what it was."

Luke thought it over for a moment. Then he began to shake his head.

"Whoops! I'm terribly sorry. I—"

"No, I don't think it's a raccoon," interrupted Luke. "I think it's something else. Maybe it's the door to the grain silo."

"No, I don't think so" replied Jenny. "The grain silo's too far away from the house for us to have heard a noise that loud. Whatever it was, it was a lot closer. Maybe one of the cats knocked something over."

Luke stood up and put on his flip flops on.

"What are you're doing?" asked Jenny.

"If it was one of the cats then I'm going outside to see what it was."

"Are you crazy?" hissed Jenny. "It's three o'clock in the morning, Luke. And you're not going out there! What if you wake Mom up?"

Luke ignored his sister and headed towards the screen door. Jenny groaned as she got on her feet and put her flip flops on.

"Maybe if you keep your voice down you won't wake Mom up," whispered Luke as Jenny joined him at the door.

"What's that supposed to mean?" she whispered back at her brother.

"Didn't you just say 'whoops?' Maybe you're the one who knocked something over."

"No, I didn't just say 'whoops,'" replied Jenny. "And I didn't knock anything over. I think you're the one who said 'whoops' and you're trying to pin it on me."

"I never said 'whoops,'" Luke argued back.

Luke and Jenny stopped and looked at one another for a moment. Finally Luke spoke up.

"Well," he whispered. "If you didn't say 'whoops,' and if I didn't say 'whoops,' then who did?"

Luke and Jenny nervously turned around and saw a young woman standing on the porch with them. She looked like she was about eighteen years old. She was slender with long dark brown hair the same color as Luke's. She wore a long blue dress with white lace trim and a little red and black hat. It looked much like the outfits they'd seen the women in Tombstone wearing back in the 1880s. She also had the same eerie white glow about her that Paul and the Swamper had. They realized she was a spirit person.

"I confess," she said as she raised her hands into the air. "I'm the one who said 'whoops.' And I'm terribly sorry. I must have knocked something over."

Luke and Jenny stood silent for a moment. Finally Jenny spoke up.

"So who are you? And what are you doing on my great grandmother's back porch?"

"Now where are my manners," she said as she stepped closer. "I should introduce myself. My name is Kate. I used to live around these parts back when Frank and Jesse James lived here."

"*You* knew the James brothers?" asked Luke. "What were they like?"

"Well, I didn't know them personally, but I certainly knew them by reputation. I overheard you talking about them during your picnic, so I decided to wait out in the cornfield until everyone else went to sleep. I've heard all about your adventures traveling back in time, so I thought I'd come and offer to take you two back to the past so you can see Frank and Jesse for yourselves."

"Word must travel fast among you spirit people," said Jenny,

Kate laughed. There was a light, almost lyrical sound to her laughter.

Then, as had happened before, a strange flash of light streaked across the sky. And the next thing they knew, Luke and Jenny were once again back in time.

Chapter Three

Quantrill's Raiders

It took Luke and Jenny a few moments to get their bearings. They looked around and found themselves standing by the side of a dirt road in the middle of a grassy plain. Kate stood nearby, and in the daylight they both noticed that she was very pretty.

"Where are we?" asked Luke.

Before anyone could answer they heard a strange sound. Almost like the sound of thunder. It was the sound of hoof beats. Many, many hoof beats. Suddenly a large group of men on horseback appeared on the horizon. It was as if an entire army was riding towards them as it looked like there were hundreds of men. But as they came closer they could see that none of the riders were wearing any military uniforms. They were racing down the road at breakneck speed. An instant later they were closing in.

"Look out, Jenny!"

Luke grabbed his sister's arm and pulled her aside. But he wasn't quite quick enough, and one of the men rode right through her.

"What the heck!" she exclaimed as she tried to regain her balance in the huge cloud of dust that was forming in the air.

"You're okay, Jenny," shouted Kate over the noise of all the running horses.

Luke and Jenny held on to each other as the band thundered past. It took some time for all of them to go by. Finally the last of the riders passed and the dust slowly began to settle.

"Your brother was trying to help you get out of the way of those men," explained Kate as they brushed away the dust, "but they can't really hurt you—"

"Because we're not really here," added Jenny. "I know. They can't see us, but we can see them."

Kate smiled as she straightened her hat.

"I see you're becoming accustomed to traveling back in time."

Luke spoke up. "Who were those guys? And how come they're all in such a big hurry?"

Kate pointed to a cloud of black smoke billowing on the horizon.

"See that?"

Luke and Jenny both nodded their heads.

"That's what's left of the town of Lawrence, Kansas. Those men who road by here were a gang called Quantrill's Raiders, and Frank James was riding with them. They've just massacred all of the men, and some of the boys, in Lawrence, and they've set the town on fire."

"Why would they do something so horrible?" asked Jenny.

"Well, Jenny, it's a very long and complicated story. If I were to try and explain everything to you we'd be here all night, in your time, that is. So I guess I'll have to give you, oh, what is it they say in your time..."

"The Reader's Digest version?" asked Luke.

"Exactly," replied Kate as she smiled and winked at Luke, "so here's the Reader's Digest version of what happened and why."

Kate began by explaining that Frank and Jesse James' parents had come to Missouri from Kentucky before the two brothers were born. And while they were still very young boys their father, Robert, decided to go to California.

"Robert James was a preacher who decided he wanted to preach the Gospel to the miners during the gold rush," explained Kate, "although there was talk that he and Zerelda were less than happily married and what he was really doing was getting away from her. He left Missouri never to return because he took sick and died shortly after he arrived in California."

"That's sad," said Jenny.

"Sounds like he got away from her for good," added Luke.

"Yes, he certainly did," agreed Kate. "But it was sad for Frank and Jesse because they never got to know their father. Perhaps if they had their lives would have turned out differently. But later on their mother married a doctor by the name of Reuben Samuels, and they settled on that farm near Kearney that your mother is taking you to visit tomorrow."

"So how do Quantrill's Raiders play into this?" asked Luke.

"I'm getting to that," replied Kate. "Frank and Jesse came of age during a very dark period in our country's history. It was the Civil War, and they found themselves in the wrong place at the wrong time."

She went on to explain that Missouri had been a slave state, but when other slave states began to secede, Missouri decided to remain neutral and part of the Union but without supporting the Union against the Confederacy.

"So wouldn't that have meant that Missouri stayed out of the war?" asked Luke.

"No, not exactly," replied Kate. "In fact, during the Civil War, Missouri turned out to be a very, very bad place to be. You see, most of the people living in Missouri, particularly in Clay County, where the James boys lived, had come from the South. Those folks were all sympathetic to the Confederacy, including Zerelda Samuels and the rest of her family. But there were other people in Missouri who came from the North, and they sided with the Union. So people in Missouri were forming their own militia groups and fighting against one another."

She went on to explain that this was called guerrilla warfare, and that it wasn't like the fighting between regular military units under the command of generals.

"Guerrilla fighters will attack both soldiers and civilians," she explained. "It's dangerous and it's ugly and all kinds of innocent folks can get hurt or killed in the process."

"Sort of like what's happening in Iraq?" asked Jenny.

"Yes," replied Kate. "From what I understand of your time, that would be a good comparison."

"Then that's not good," said Luke shaking his head.

"No, it certainly wasn't," replied Kate.

She went on to explain that in Missouri people on both sides of the war were doing many, many horrible things to one another. They were attacking and killing each other, burning down one another's homes and taking away each other's property.

"There really is nothing civil about a civil war," she added. "In fact, all civility goes out the window because law and order breaks down as people do terrible things to their neighbors and their fellow countrymen. And they weren't doing this just to other Missourians. They were fighting with folks in Kansas and other states too."

"So what about the regular army?" asked Luke.

"Oh, there were pro-Union forces involved in it too," said Kate, "which probably helped make it even worse. And it was all this chaos, and all this horror, that made it easy for a man like William Clarke Quantrill to come along and wreak even more havoc."

"Who was William Clarke Quantrill?" asked Jenny.

"Quantrill was really nothing more than a war criminal," replied Kate.

She explained that Quantrill originally came from Ohio, that he was a schoolteacher at one time, and maybe even a preacher for a time as well. He had formed his own militia band and they were called Quantrill's Raiders. They were raiding and looting parts of Kansas and even went as far south as Texas and Arkansas. And when Frank James became one of Quantrill's Raiders, he met and befriended a man by the name of Cole Younger.

"I've heard of him," said Luke. "Weren't the Younger brothers and the James brothers all outlaws together?"

"Indeed they were," replied Kate. "I suppose you could say that their outlaw days really began when Frank and Cole rode with Quantrill's Raiders."

"So what happened in Lawrence?" asked Jenny.

Kate went on to tell them that during the summer of 1863 a Union general by the name of Thomas Ewing had been ordered to stop the guerillas. He decided the best way to get to Quantrill's Raiders would be by going after members of their families. He was arresting and jailing the wives, mothers and sisters of the Quantrill men, and he was holding the ladies prisoner in a three-story building in Kansas City. He had so many of them imprisoned there that the floors of the building actually collapsed and many of the women inside ended up either seriously hurt or killed.

"But I didn't think anyone could throw you in jail because of something someone else in your family did," argued Jenny.

"No, you really can't throw someone in jail for something another member of their family does, unless, of course, they helped out the person doing the wrong," explained Kate. "But you have to remember it was a time of war and their menfolk were enemies of the Union, even if they weren't in the regular Confederate army. Still, I really don't think General Ewing ever meant for any of the ladies to be harmed. I'm sure his intention was to let them go once the men surrendered."

She went on to tell them that after this happened rumors came back to the Quantrill men that General Ewing had done this to the ladies on purpose, so the Raiders decided they were going to get even by attacking the town of Lawrence, Kansas. Lawrence was the home of another Confederate enemy. He was pro-Union commander and a United States Senator by the name of James Lane. General Lane had led attacks against civilians in Missouri, and he and his men had recently looted and burned the town of Osceola, Missouri, killing innocent people there as well.

Kate sighed and paused for a moment as she pointed back to the black cloud of smoke on the horizon. As the three gazed upon it she went on with her story. She told them that on August 21,1863, William Clarke Quantrill and some 450 men committed the worst civilian massacre of the entire Civil War. They began their attack around dawn, and for the next two hours they hunted down and murdered about 150 defenseless men and boys. But the man they wanted the most, Senator Lane, fled upon hearing the Raiders' rebel yell as they stormed into town. He hid in a cornfield, wearing only his nightshirt, and somehow managed to not be found by the Raiders.

"Did they ever get him?" asked Luke.

"No," replied Kate. "But he would die by his own hand after the war. Perhaps it was out of guilt for the Lawrence massacre."

"What about the women and girls?" asked Jenny.

"None of the women or girls were harmed, but they were forced to watch their husbands and fathers, brothers and sons all be brutally murdered."

The three stood in silence for a moment to take it all in. Then Jenny spoke up.

"That's horrible. Did Quantrill kill any children?"

Kate nodded.

"How young were the children he murdered?"

"Some of them were probably less than ten."

Jenny was appalled.

"That means they were the same age as me and my little brother! So how does killing little kids bring back the people Senator Lane killed in Missouri?"

"It doesn't," said Kate.

"Our parents always say that two wrongs don't make a right," said Luke.

"That's right, Luke," agreed Kate. "Two wrongs never ever make a right! Especially when you're talking about intentionally harming innocent people. And if killing the men and boys wasn't enough, Quantrill and his men began burning down people's homes too, some of which had people still hiding inside."

She went on to say that after they finished their butchery they decided to celebrate their dirty deed by looting the saloons and getting drunk. But by around 9 o'clock in the morning the Union forces began showing up so the Raiders headed back to Missouri.

"So that's who all those guys were that just rode past us," said Jenny.

Kate nodded.

"Was Jesse James with them too?" asked Jenny.

"No, Jesse was still living at home at the time this happened."

"Can you take us to Lawrence so we can see it?" asked Luke.

"No, I'm afraid not. The scene over there right now is far worse than anything you could possibly imagine. You'd never be able to get back to sleep afterwards and then later on you would probably have nightmares."

Luke looked disappointed.

"Oh, don't worry, Luke, you'll be seeing plenty of action

20

real soon," assured Kate.

She went on to tell them that Quantrill's Raiders would split up, at least for a time, once they returned to Missouri. Only a few involved in the massacre would ever be captured by the Union forces, but those who were would end up being executed for their crimes.

"And then what happened?" asked Jenny.

Kate explained that the Civil War would go on for another two years, and during that time many people in Missouri would be banished from their homes and farms. Jesse James and his family were being harassed by pro-Union forces back home on their farm, and at one point Mrs. Samuels and one or more of her other children were arrested and jailed for a time as well. This angered young Jesse so much that he decided to join his older brother Frank in the militia.

As Kate was speaking the grassy plain began to fade away and Luke and Jenny suddenly found themselves at a railroad depot.

Chapter Four
Jesse Joins the Militia

As Luke and Jenny looked around the railroad depot Kate began telling them about another militia leader, Bill Anderson.

"They called him Bloody Bill Anderson," she explained. She went on to say that Anderson had also rode with Quantrill for a time, but now he was leading his own band of guerillas.

"No one seems to know exactly where or when Jesse James joined the militia, but it was sometime in 1864 that young Jesse was riding with Bloody Bill, because that's when he was very seriously injured. It was in the middle of August, as I recall."

"What happened?" asked Luke. "Did Jesse James get shot?"

"That's what they say," replied Kate. "Seems that young Jesse tried to steal a horse and a farmer caught him in the act and shot him. Other folks say he was wounded fighting the cavalry at Fort Rock Ford." She shrugged her shoulders. "Who's to say? So much of what folks hear about the James boys is more legend than actual fact. But what I do know for certain is after he got hurt they didn't think he would live, but he did, although it left him with a scar on the right side of his chest."

Suddenly they heard a noise outside. Once again, it was the thunder of many hoof beats, followed by the horrible sound of people screaming in terror. They ran outside the depot and discovered themselves in a little town. A band of ragged-looking men with long dirty beards and wearing dirty coats was riding up and down the street. Kate told them they were now in Centralia, Missouri, and that the riders were none other than Bloody Bill Anderson and his men. Luke and Jenny watched in horror as what seemed like hundreds of men began terrorizing the townspeople. They were attacking men, women and even children and looting the two stores in town. Then Luke pointed out a couple of the men who were rolling barrels of whiskey away from the stores and onto the street. Once they set the barrels upright they opened them and began drinking. Soon their friends came to join them, and before long they were all getting drunk.

"This is not good!" exclaimed Luke.

"No it isn't," replied Kate. "These men are bad enough when they're sober, but when they're drunk they're even more ruthless."

"Look out, Luke!" exclaimed Jenny.

Some of the men were riding up to the depot, and they rushed in so quickly that Jenny barely had time to pull Luke away.

"I won't get hurt, you know!"

"That's Bloody Bill himself," said Kate, pointing out the mean-looking man with a messy black beard who was approaching the depot. As he walked past Jenny he came so close to her that his coat brushed through her sweatshirt.

She looked over her shoulder and noticed Bloody Bill

23

reading a sign posted on the depot wall. A few of his men joined him and they began mumbling something about when the next train would be coming. She then turned back to her brother and Kate. Anderson's men were still terrorizing the town. She felt so sorry for the townspeople and wished there was something she could do to make it stop. Moments later she caught the whiff of something strange in the air.

"Do you smell smoke?"

Her brother nodded. They spun back around to see that Anderson's men had just set the depot on fire.

"Funny, but I don't feel the heat," remarked Jenny as they stepped away from the depot.

Flames began engulfing the building. Before long it turned into a blazing inferno.

"Jenny, look over there!"

Jenny turned to where Luke was pointing. A stagecoach was approaching.

"What do you think will happen to them?" asked Luke.

"I don't know," she replied. "Those poor people have no idea what kind of trouble they're in."

They watched as some of Anderson's men rode up to meet the stagecoach. As soon as the driver halted the coach they could hear the men shouting at the passengers and ordering them out of the stagecoach. As soon as the last passenger stepped off, one of Anderson's men robbed them at gunpoint while the others looted the stagecoach. A few of the passengers tried arguing with the robbers, saying they were for the Confederacy, but it didn't seem to matter to any of Anderson's men. They robbed and bullied all of the frightened passengers just like they were doing to the townspeople.

"Why would they go and do something like that?" asked Luke. "None of those people are soldiers, so where's the battle?"

"It's the time these people live in," explained Kate. "No one's safe because there's no justice anymore. Law and order has completely broken down, and criminals, like Quantrill and Bloody Bill, are using the war as an excuse to commit their crimes."

The chaos continued and a short time later they heard the whistle of a train, but it never made it to the depot. By then some of Anderson's men had blocked the track with a pile of railroad ties. And, just as had happened with the stagecoach, when the train slowed to a halt some of the men rode up to meet it with their guns blazing.

"Kind of reminds me of a scene out of a Western movie," said Jenny as Luke nodded his head in agreement.

They watched Anderson's men force the frightened passengers off the train. They too were all robbed at gunpoint, just as the stagecoach passengers had been.

"Uh-oh," said Luke as a small group of Union soldiers got off the train. "This isn't going to be good."

The soldiers were quickly taken aside from the other passengers and forced to strip down to undergarments. Kate explained that the guerrillas would have wanted the uniforms so they could disguise themselves. Once the men were out of their uniforms Bloody Bill approached them.

"All right," he shouted, "I want to know who among you is an officer."

One man stepped forward.

"I am. My name is Tom Goodman."

"Who's your commanding officer?"

"General Sherman. My men and I are on leave."

"Sherman!" bellowed Bloody Bill.

Kate explained that General Sherman and his men had recently burned the city of Atlanta. That meant they would have been especially hated by Southerners and anyone else who supported the Confederacy.

Anderson looked back at the small group of his men who stood nearby.

"Clement?"

"Yes sir," replied a young man as he stepped forward.

"I think it's about time to parole these soldiers."

Clement began to laugh as he waved to his friends to join him. They quickly lined up the soldiers.

"Sir! Wait!" shouted one of the passengers. "You've gotten what you wanted from us. Can we go now? We're only going as far as Sturgeon, and that's just up the line."

Stunned silence fell. The air was thick with tension. No one knew what Bloody Bill would do next. Luke and Jenny braced themselves as they watched. It seemed like forever before Bloody Bill faced down the passengers.

"You can go to blazes(is this the word you want to use?) for all I care," he calmly replied.

With that Bloody Bill turned his back and casually stepped away. And as he walked towards Luke and Jenny his men began setting the train on fire.

"They sure have a thing about burning stuff," said Luke.

"Let's go," said Kate, "we've seen enough here."

"Why? What's going on?"

"Don't argue with me, Luke," said Kate. "We're leaving—now!"

Within an instant Luke and Jenny found themselves walking down a country road just outside of town. They could hear the sound of gunshots behind them, followed by the blood-chilling sound of people screaming in terror.

"The man you saw lining up those soldiers was Little Archie Clement, the Executioner of Centralia," explained Kate. "And after he lined up those unarmed soldiers he and the others executed them, one by one, in cold blood."

"I had a feeling that something really bad was going to happen once they separated those soldiers from the rest of the passengers," said Jenny.

"I guess that's why they called their leader Bloody Bill," added Luke.

"Yes indeed," said Kate. "But you see, General William Tecumseh Sherman is a man badly hated in the South because he not only captures cities like Atlanta, he burns them to the ground. And that means he makes women and children and old people suffer as well, just like Quantrill does. It's like I said before – both sides are guilty of doing horrible things to one another."

As they kept walking down the road the sounds of the gunfire eventually stopped. A short time later Bloody Bill and his men thundered past, and Luke and Jenny could see the Union sergeant, Goodman, riding with them. Bloody Bill had taken the man prisoner for some reason, but what cruel fate may have awaited him they did not know and they were afraid to ask. Kate went on to explain that Union troops would arrive in Centralia later on that afternoon. They would try to hunt down Bloody Bill Anderson, but Bloody Bill would escape, at least this time.

"Did they ever catch him?" asked Jenny.

"Yes, they did. He was killed about a month or so later after this happened in an ambush. Jesse James would be with him at the time, but he would manage to escape."

"Is this how Jesse James became an outlaw?" asked Luke.

"Yes, Luke. William Clarke Quantrill and Bloody Bill Anderson were mighty fine teachers. They taught Frank and Jesse James, and Cole Younger, how to become master criminals."

Chapter Five
Quantrill's Ghost

For a long time no one spoke. Luke, Jenny and Kate walked down the road in silence. They watched Bloody Bill Anderson and his men ride further and further away. The sound of their horses' hoof beats grew softer and softer. Before long they were just dots on the horizon which slowly disappeared. And even though they knew that in the end Bloody Bill would pay for his crimes, it didn't lift their spirits. Even Kate seemed at a loss for words. Finally Jenny spoke up and broke the silence.

"You know, we studied the Civil War last year in my social studies class, and it was nothing like this."

No one responded.

"At school they made it all seem so boring. All my teacher ever talked about was names and dates and President Lincoln getting shot and Robert E. Lee and all that other stuff. And all I ever thought about was that lunch period was right after social studies class and that meant I could go hang out with my friends for awhile. I never really thought about all the people who got hurt and killed in such an awful way. Now I feel really bad."

"No need to," replied Kate. "Unfortunately, that's the way the schools teach history, Jenny. And I agree, there is a whole lot more to history than just names and dates. History is about real people and why they did the things they did. But not everyone gets to go out and experience it like you and your brother do."

Kate went on to explain that though the Civil War would end in 1865, it would take many, many years for the wounds to heal.

"Despite what your politicians and news people may tell you about the events of your time, the Civil War really was the worst thing that ever happened to us as a country. Things like this stay in people's memories for a long, long time, and they pass on all the stories about what happened to them to their children, and to their children's children. Sometimes all that anger and resentment never really goes away."

"I know," said Luke. "I remember my dad telling me that there are places around our country today where people still talk about the Civil War."

"And where they still say the South will rise again," added Jenny.

"Exactly," said Kate. "That's what I meant when I said that sometimes that anger and resentment never really goes away. It just keeps getting passed down from one generation to the next."

"Kind of like in Iraq?" asked Luke.

"I think so," replied his sister. "From what Dad says in some of his e-mails, I think that's what he means too."

The three walked in silence for a time again until Jenny spoke up once more.

"What about you, Kate? You seem awfully quiet. Is this bringing up bad memories for you too?"

"Yes and no." She paused for a moment. "I was born in December of 1866, a little over a year after the Civil War ended, so I don't have any memories of it myself. Seeing some of this has been a bit of a shock for me too. My father and his brothers—my uncles, and most of the other menfolk in my family—all came from Tennessee, so they fought for the Confederacy. But my mother's family came from Ohio so I had uncles and cousins who lived there and fought for the Union. I grew up listening to their stories and hearing all about it. I even lost an uncle at Gettysburg, and another uncle lost his leg after being wounded there. And I lost a few cousins in some of the other battles too."

"So how would you have known Frank and Jesse James? I mean, known about them?" asked Luke.

"Frank and Jesse were famous outlaws for about seventeen years, so I grew up hearing all about them too. During their day everybody knew all about Frank and Jesse James. They were in all the papers, and there were even dime novels written about them too."

"Dime novels?" asked Jenny.

"That's what we used to call those little paperback books that were so popular in my day. They usually cost a dime and there were all kinds of dime novels published about Frank and Jesse James, although I think most of them were probably more legend than fact. And with those dime novels I suspect that folks across the sea in places like England and France probably heard all about Frank and Jesse James too."

"What's *that?*" asked Jenny.

She pointed to a strange cloud of mist forming in the road in front of them. The three suddenly stopped in their tracks.

"I don't like the looks of this," said Kate.

The cloud of mist grew bigger and thicker. After a few moments a man stepped out. He was very handsome. He appeared to be about thirty years old and he had dark, wavy hair and a dark handlebar mustache. He was well dressed in a fine looking business suit and top hat, and he had the same eerie white glow about him that Kate had. He looked at the two youngsters and smiled as he bowed and tipped his hat to Jenny.

"How do you do, young lady? I am very pleased to meet you, my dear."

"Who are you?"

"Jenny!" exclaimed Kate. "Whatever you do, *do not* talk to this man!"

"Now, Miss Kate, where are your manners? I'm not here to make any trouble. I just wanted to introduce myself to these two fine young people."

Before Kate could reply Jenny took a few steps towards the handsome stranger.

"He seems nice enough to me."

"That's right, my dear. I really am a very nice man. Did you know that I used to be a schoolteacher? I just overheard you talking about your social studies class. And I'll bet I would have been much more interesting than your social studies teacher was. What was your teacher's name, dear?"

"Mrs. Sullivan."

"Jenny!" exclaimed Kate.

But Jenny ignored her. It was as if this handsome stranger had cast some sort of a spell on her. She just couldn't turn away from him.

"Now you trusted Mrs. Sullivan, didn't you?"

Jenny nodded.

"Sure. She was my teacher."

"Well, then, if you can trust her than you can trust me too. Because I would like to be your teacher too, if you don't mind."

"Jenny! No!" shouted Kate. "I said don't—"

"And my name is Mr. Quantrill," said the man, cutting off Kate's warning.

He reached over and grabbed Jenny by the wrist, pulling her closer to him. He looked into her eyes with a cold, hard stare.

"And everything you've just learned about me is wrong!"

"Please let go of me," begged Jenny.

"Let go of her, Quantrill!" demanded Kate in a very stern voice.

"Now, Kate, you know I mean the girl no harm. But I've been slandered here, and I've come to set the record straight."

"I don't think so," said Luke. "We heard all about what you did to all those people in Lawrence, Kansas. You even killed kids just like me while you were there! And we saw all the smoke in the sky from it too. Now you let go of my sister!"

Luke took a couple of steps toward Quantrill, but Kate called out to him and told him to stay back. Luke froze in his tracks.

"Those men were our enemies!" bellowed Quantrill. "And I was right to do what I did!" He looked back down at Jenny. "Wasn't I?"

Jenny did not respond. She turned her head to look back at Kate. She looked very scared. Quantrill reached down and grabbed her by the chin, forcing her to look up at him. She could see that his eyes were black with rage.

"Y-yes. You were right." She spoke very softly, almost in a whisper.

"That's right, my dear," replied Quantrill. His voice was much calmer, but icy cold. "I was right to do what I did, and now I'm going to prove it to you."

Quantrill held on to Jenny's chin, forcing her to keep looking into his eyes. Suddenly they turned bright red. Then his face slowly melted into a skull. Jenny screamed.

"Calm down, Jenny!" shouted Kate. "He feeds on your fear!"

She turned back to Quantrill and spoke calmly to him.

"All right, you've had your fun. We all see that you

32

can frighten a little girl. But it doesn't change the fact that you're not as smart or as brave of a leader as you claim to be. Does Walkfield's farm in Kentucky sound familiar to you? The way I hear it you were gunned down in your sleep by Union troops who were able to sneak up on you and your men while you slept in the barn. I have the upper hand here, sir, and you know it."

Quantrill looked at Kate. His skull and red eyes slowly melted back into the handsome face they had seen before. He smiled sheepishly and let go of Jenny's chin but still held fast to her wrist.

"Now, Miss Kate, you know I meant the girl no harm. I simply wanted her to hear my side of the story."

He paused, but he could see Kate was unmoved, so he tried changing the subject.

"Kate. My dear, that is indeed such a lovely name. Did you know that my sweetheart's name was also Kate?"

Kate did not respond. And before Quantrill could say anything more a strange light streaked across the sky. Luke and Jenny suddenly found themselves back on Great Grandmother Katie's screened-in back porch. Kate stood nearby, and she did not look pleased.

"Am I in trouble?" asked Jenny.

"Keep your voice down before you wake the others," hissed Kate. "And yes, you're in trouble, young lady. When I tell you not to do something I mean it."

"I'm sorry," said Jenny.

Kate's voice softened.

"Look, Jenny, I know you've been taught not to talk to strangers, and the same rule applies here. There are good spirit people and bad spirit people, just like there are good and bad flesh-and-blood people. That man was a very, very bad man in life, and he is still a bad man in death."

"Is he going to come back and try to get me again?"

"No," replied Kate. "I've brought you back to your time and he can't find you here."

"Where is he now?"

"He's gone back to where he came from. He won't be bothering you again."

"Does this mean we're done?" asked Luke. "We didn't even get to see Frank or Jesse James."

Kate looked back and forth at the two youngsters.

"Well now, that's really up to the two of you. Are you going to do what I tell you from here on out?"

Both Luke and Jenny nodded.

"Okay, then we'll go back. But if either one of you gives me anymore trouble we're done. Understood?"

The two nodded their heads. Then Luke nudged his sister's shoulder and whispered in her ear.

"She sounds just like Mom."

Kate looked at Luke and laughed.

"What's so funny?"

"Oh nothing, Luke. Not a thing."

A second later they found themselves back in time again. They were standing by a creek in the middle of the woods, and over the sound of the running water they could barely make out a strange sound.

Chapter Six

Buck and Dingus

"Luke? Do you hear that?" asked Jenny.

"What?"

"Shh!"

She paused for a moment.

"That. Did you hear it?"

Luke stood still. He could hear the sound of the water gushing down the creek. Then, as he listened carefully, he could barely hear another faint sound. It sounded like someone moaning.

"Yeah," he replied, nodding his head. "Now I hear it."

He waited for the sound to come again.

"I think it came from over there," he said, pointing downstream from where they were standing.

Luke and Jenny took off towards the strange sound. Kate followed close behind. They soon found what they were looking for. A young teenaged boy was lying in the creek bed. They could see he had a bullet wound on the right side of his chest. He must have been seriously injured. His face was pale, his skin looked clammy, and he was bleeding very badly.

"Who is he?" asked Jenny.

"That's Jesse James," replied Kate. "He and a few of his fellow guerrillas were on their way to surrender, but along the way they ran into some drunken Union soldiers who fired on them."

"But I thought you said the war was over," said Luke.

"It is, and no one knows for sure exactly how this happened. I recall hearing something about the Union forces still hunting for Archie Clement, the man who executed all those soldiers from that train back in Centralia. Maybe this was a case of mistaken identity or a breakdown in communication."

As Kate was talking Jesse began slowly crawling away from the creek.

"I feel so helpless," said Jenny. "I wish I could go get help."

"Help is soon on the way," said Kate.

She went on to say that this wound was near the scar on Jesse's chest leftover from when he had been shot the year before. This one too would leave him with a scar. After a few agonizing minutes Jesse managed to crawl away from the creek. They could see a farm hand plowing a nearby field.

"Over here!" shouted Luke. "This man needs help!"

"He can't hear you," reminded Kate.

Jesse somehow managed to get the man's attention. He quickly came to the scene, gathered the young man up and carried him to a nearby farmhouse. Luke, Jenny and Kate followed along. He knocked on the door and a woman in a blue gingham dress soon answered.

"Oh my lord. What happened?"

"I found him while I was out plowing the field, Mrs. Bradley. He's hurt real bad. I don't think he's gonna make it."

"Here, bring him inside. Quickly!"

They followed the man inside the house and watched

as he gently eased Jesse down on a nearby bed. As the lady tended to his wounds Kate explained that he would indeed make a full recovery, but it would be a long time coming. He would remain at the Bradley home until he was well enough to travel, then he would ride in the back of a wagon to Lexington with his friends to surrender. Afterwards he would be returned home to his family.

"While Frank and Jesse were away fighting the war Mrs. Samuels and the rest of the family were taken from their home near Kearney and sent away to Nebraska," explained Kate. "And Jesse had been so seriously wounded that for a time even he didn't think he would make it, and he told his mother that he didn't want to die in Nebraska."

She went on to say that the story went that when a Union officer, Captain Rogers, heard of the family's exile he arranged for them to travel back to Missouri by steamboat. There, in a town called Harlem, Jesse would recover at the home of his uncle and aunt, John and Mary James Mimms.

Within an instant Luke, Jenny and Kate found themselves in another home. They saw young Jesse lying in another bed. He looked much better. The color had returned to his face and, for the first time, they noticed what a handsome young man he was. He had dark hair with fine chiseled features and high cheekbones.

"He's hot," said Jenny. "He looks like a rock star. I'll bet if he lived in my time he could have been an actor."

While she was admiring Jesse's good looks a pretty young girl with long dark curly hair entered the room to check on him. Jesse's face lit up as soon as he saw her.

"Hello, Zee," he said with a big smile.

The girl looked happy to see him too. She leaned down and kissed Jesse on the cheek. As they watched her tend to him Kate explained that she was the Mimms' daughter and her name was also Zerelda, the same as Jesse's mother, and she went by the nickname Zee. Kate also told them that

37

Jesse was in love with her.

"But if her parents were Jesse's uncle and aunt, doesn't that make them cousins?" asked Jenny.

"Yes," replied Kate, "they were indeed cousins. But you have to realize that sometimes cousins do marry."

"Really?" asked Jenny.

"Why yes," replied Kate. "Over in England, Queen Victoria was married to her cousin, Prince Albert. He passed away a few years ago; the poor Queen never fully recovered from her loss. So indeed, cousins sometimes do fall in love and marry, and Jesse and Zee will marry someday, but not for many years from now."

It was almost as if Jesse had heard her. He reached for Zee's hand.

"Someday, Zee, when times are better, I swear I'm going to make you my wife."

Kate went on to explain that while this was happening Jesse's older brother, Frank, had also surrendered. The family would very soon return to their farm near Kearney where they would all be reunited. And once they were all back home Frank would help his stepfather rebuild their farm while Jesse recovered.

"Did either of the James brothers or their friends have to go to jail for what they did in the war?" asked Jenny.

"No," said Kate. "I don't have time to explain all the details of the how and why, but after the war ended most of the men who had served in the militias, including the James brothers, were allowed to return home and resume their lives. No doubt some of them went back to farms and their families and tried to put their lives back together as best they could. But even with the war now behind them, many of them were restless and unhappy."

"But if the war was over wouldn't that have meant that we were all Americans again?" asked Jenny. "Wouldn't people have put their differences aside and worked together to rebuild the country?"

"If only it could have been that simple, Jenny," replied Kate. "After the war ended people were hardly united. Let me see if I can explain it using the lingo of your times."

She paused for a moment to gather her thoughts.

"It was as if the Northerners had said to us, 'We won, you lost, and now we're going to make you pay for it.'"

She went on to say that because their side had lost the war former Confederates and Confederate sympathizers felt very bitter. Many had lost everything they had. Some had even lost their entire families. She reminded them that Clay County was in an area of western Missouri that had been called the burning district because so many homes and farms had been destroyed during the war. That meant many of the former militiamen would have had nothing left to return to. Their problems would be made even worse as Union banks and Yankee businessmen moved into the area and set up shop. They would make life even more difficult for the people of Missouri. They would take away people's land, squeeze out the local businesses, and even take away people's bank accounts.

"They were called Carpetbaggers," explained Kate, "because they would arrive with their traveling carpetbags."

"Like a suitcase?" asked Jenny.

"Yes," replied Kate. "And the way most of the former Confederates saw it, they were coming here to loot and plunder the state of Missouri just as they were doing with other former Confederate states."

She went on to say that such hard times and harsh political climate meant lawlessness would become a real problem in Missouri for many years to come after the Civil War. And as a result all the hardships placed upon them many of these former militiamen would end up becoming outlaws, including Frank and Jesse James. Or, as their close friends called them, Buck and Dingus.

Chapter Seven

The Liberty Bank Robbery

Luke and Jenny looked back at young Jesse James, who by this time had raised himself up on the bed and was happily chatting away with his cousin Zee. It was hard to believe this nice looking young man would one day become a famous and notorious outlaw.

"Eeew, gross!"

"What is it, Jenny?" asked Kate.

"Look! There! At his hand!" Jenny was pointing to Jesse's left hand. "Part of his finger is missing."

"Yes indeed," replied Kate. "Jesse lost the top part of his middle finger."

"How did that happen?" asked Luke.

"He lost it by accident while handling a pistol, but I don't know all the details of exactly how it happened," replied Kate. "And I believe that's what earned him the nickname Dingus. So let that be a lesson to you that firearms must always be handled with great care. And that missing fingertip will prove to be important later on too. But for now it's time for us to go."

The next thing the two youngsters knew they were walking the streets of another little town. It looked like the set of a Western movie and it reminded them of when they went back in time in Tombstone. But unlike Tombstone there was snow covering the ground. The few people on the streets wore heavy coats and the sky looked silvery, as if it would soon start to snow again. Luke and Jenny were glad they couldn't feel the cold. Still, they couldn't help but shiver in their sweat clothes. As they strolled the streets Kate told them they were in a little town called Liberty, Missouri.

Moments later a band of about a dozen men rode by. They were wearing bits and pieces of Union uniforms. Luke wondered if maybe they might have been Union soldiers during the war. As they entered the town the group broke up and took up positions around one of the buildings—the Clay County Savings Bank. Then, as if on cue, two of the men stopped and dismounted their horses. They tried to look as casual as they could while they entered the Clay County Savings Bank. Kate motioned Luke and Jenny to follow them inside.

Upon entering the bank they found two men working at their desks. One of the men appeared to be much older than the other. It was very quiet as there were no other customers inside the bank. The two workers looked up and saw one of the men walk up to the wood stove trying to warm himself up while the other walked up to the counter and pulled a bill out of his pocket.

"Would one of you mind breaking this for me?"

"Certainly, sir," replied the younger man as he rose from his desk. But as he approached his customer he was stunned to see the man draw his gun and point it in his face.

"Give me all your money! NOW! Or else I'll kill the both of you. Here and now."

"Don't argue with him, son," said the older bank

worker, as the other robber walked up to him and put a gun to his head. "Just do what he tells you to do."

"But father—"

"Just do as he says," said the older man.

"Your old man's giving you some good advice, *son,*" said the robber. "Now you and me are going to take a little walk. Over there."

The robber pointed to the door of the bank vault. The young man hesitated. He looked back at his father, and the older man nodded his head. Even though he was being held at gunpoint he managed to remain calm.

The young man signed as he opened the bank vault and led the robber inside. With shaking hands he placed all the bank's money in a sack. The robber stood close by and watched his every move. asOnce he finished emptying the vault his father was shoved into it with him. The robbers closed the vault door and fled the bank.

"Are we leaving now?" asked Luke.

"Not yet," replied Kate.

A few moments later the vault door slowly opened and the two men cautiously peeked out and looked around. Once they realized the robbers were gone they scrambled to the windows.

"Help! We've been robbed! Stop those men!"

Kate rushed Luke and Jenny outside. They saw the two robbers were about to mount their horses. The shouts of the men inside the bank alerted two other young men who stood across the street.

"Don't move!" shouted one of the robbers.

Before either of the two men could respond one of the bandits fired at them, hitting one of them. As he tumbled to the ground his friend knelt down beside him. Seconds later the two fired a shot at another passer-by. As they got back on their horses their friends rode up to join them. They shouted a rebel yell as they raced away on their horses.

"You just witnessed a real moment in history," explained

Kate. "This is the very first time a bank has ever been robbed during peacetime in broad daylight."

She went on to say that the two men across the street from the bank were a couple of college students, and the one who was hit was killed.

"Was Jesse one of the robbers?" asked Jenny.

"No one knows for certain, but I doubt it," replied Kate. "Jesse still hasn't fully recovered from his wound yet. But a lot of folks believe the two men who went inside the bank were Frank James and his friend Cole Younger."

As she was speaking a number of men began gathering to form a posse. They shouted back and forth to one another as they gathered in the street and mounted their horses. Other townspeople came out and tried to help the young man who had been shot. Within minutes the posse was racing out of town after the robbers. And as they rode away snowflakes began to fall.

"Were any of them caught?" asked Luke.

"No," replied Kate. "They rode off towards the Missouri River and took a ferry across. By the time the posse reached the ferry the snowstorm had erased their tracks."

"Did they find out who did it?" asked Jenny.

"Not exactly. It's generally believed that all robbers were former Quantrill men, and that along with Frank and Cole, Jim Younger was also involved. It was the beginning of an era. The James and Younger brothers would be robbing banks for many years to come."

Chapter Eight
The Russellville Bank Robbery

Luke, Jenny and Kate stayed underneath one of the building awnings and watched the snow as it fell. Having lived in the Arizona desert all their lives falling snow was something they'd never seen. To them it was fascinating.

"The rest of the 1860s and the 1870s would be a time of lawlessness for the people of Missouri," explained Kate as they watched the snow drifting higher and higher. "There would be many more armed robberies in many other towns just like this one. It's believed that most, if not all, of the robberies were committed by former Quantrill and Anderson men. And it's generally thought that Frank and Jesse James, along with Cole Younger and his brothers, were involved one way or another in just about all of them, but it's hard to know for sure exactly how and when."

"How come?" asked Luke.

"Well, let's face it. Having a gun suddenly shoved in your face is a very scary thing," replied Kate. "Most folks who were robbed were probably so shook up that it was hard for them to remember much of anything else but the sight of that gun barrel. And besides, it was a different time. We didn't have all those fancy gadgets that you have in your time that record everything."

"You mean video cameras?" asked Jenny.

"Yes, whatever it is that you call them. I hear that in your time those gadgets take pictures of the robbers while they're doing the deed. But we sure didn't have anything even close to that back then. If we had, I'm sure Frank and Jesse's careers would have ended much sooner."

She went on to say that when they weren't committing robberies the James and Younger brothers did a lot of traveling. In the summer of 1867 Jesse took a trip to Tennessee to visit a doctor who would treat his lung; the one that had been injured when he was shot. On the way home he stopped in Kentucky where he met up with his brother, Frank, who was traveling with Cole Younger. Frank and Cole went on to New York City, and along the way they cashed some of the bonds taken in the Liberty Bank robbery. From there Frank journeyed to California. He wanted to find out more about his father's life there and visit his father's grave, although he never found it. Afterwards he worked for a time at a ranch in San Luis Obispo. Frank thought the California climate might be good for Jesse's health so he wrote Jesse a letter suggesting he come and join him. Jesse agreed, but there was a problem. He didn't have the money to take a trip that far. So the two brothers agreed to meet Cole Younger in Kentucky to discuss a business venture.

"In other words, they were gonna rob another bank," said Luke.

"Exactly," said Kate. "And what makes this particular one so unusual is the bank they decided to rob. It was in Russellville, Kentucky. It was called the Nimrod Long Banking Company. One of the bank's owners, Mr. Long, had helped to fund their father's college scholarship when he was a young man studying to become a minister at Georgetown College in Kentucky."

"You mean they were going to rob someone who had helped their father?" asked Jenny.

"Yes," replied Kate.

"Well that's not a very nice thing to do, is it?"

"It's a good thing their father wasn't there to see it," added Luke. "I don't think he would have been very proud of them for doing something like that."

"Indeed he wasn't," said Kate.

Within the blink of an eye they found themselves in another western town. But this time there were only a few small patches of snow on the ground. It must have been springtime. The buds on the trees were starting to bloom.

"Are we in Russellville?" asked Luke.

"Uh-huh," replied Kate, pointing to the building across the street. "And over there is the Nimrod Long Banking Company."

As the three crossed the street Kate explained that a week earlier one of the robbers had entered the bank. He said his name was Thomas Colburn and that he was visiting from Louisville. He asked Mr. Long to exchange a bond, but Mr. Long got suspicious and refused. He returned a few days later with another man and asked to cash a one hundred dollar note. But Mr. Long didn't like the looks of Mr. Colburn's friend, so he again said no.

Just as they were about to enter the bank three men stepped in front of them and opened the door. Luke, Jenny and Kate followed them inside where they spotted two bank employees having their lunch. A third bank employee stood nearby.

"Look, Mr. Long. It's Mr. Colburn again," said one of the employees.

The man he was pointing at stepped up to the bank counter next to where Mr. Long was standing. He threw down a fifty-dollar bill.

"So, is my money still not good enough for this bank's president?"

Mr. Long glanced down at the bill.

"I think this is counterfeit money, and I'm not going

to cash it."

Mr. Colburn reached into his coat and pulled out a revolver. He shoved the barrel into the bank president's face. The other two men quickly drew their guns too.

"In that case, you're going to give me all this bank's money. Now!"

Mr. Long tried to escape. He turned and rushed toward the back door as a fourth robber entered through a side door with his gun drawn as well.

"I'd stop right there if I were you," he said.

Mr. Long ignored the robber's demands and kept running for the back door. Then Mr. Colburn fired his gun. The bullet grazed the side of Mr. Long's head and he fell to the ground. Colburn, who was following closely behind, hit Mr. Long on the head with his gun when the man fell. But seconds later, when he turned back to see what his friends were doing, Mr. Long got back up, and this time he was able to flee out the back door.

Once safely outside Mr. Long ignored his bleeding head and ran to the front of the bank, calling for help. But when he reached the bank's front door he found two other men waiting there on horseback. Luke and Jenny watched through the front windows as the two men quickly drew their guns and began to open fire on him.

"Sometimes it just isn't your day," said Jenny.

"Now, are you two going to cooperate with us or not?" asked Mr. Colburn.

The two other bank employees slowly nodded their heads as they were held at gunpoint. They watched helplessly as the robbers loaded up their sacks with cash.

Kate told explained that the robbers got over fourteen thousand dollars.

"Wow!" exclaimed Luke. "Even in our time that's a lot of money."

The three followed the robbers out the front door and watched them as they mounted their horses and started to ride away. One of the townsmen tried shooting at the robbers, but they returned fire and the man was killed.

"I see what you mean, Kate," said Jenny. "So much was happening so fast in there that I just didn't get a good look at the robbers."

"Neither did I," said Luke.

"It's generally believed that Mr. Colburn was actually Cole Younger," said Kate, "and Frank James may have been one of the two men who came into the bank with him."

She went on to say that one of the robbers would later be arrested by the authorities and sent to prison. Another would be shot and killed while resisting arrest, but the James brothers and Cole Younger were not with either one when they were caught. In fact they would all deny they had anything do with the Russellville bank robbery, just as they had denied anything to do with any of the other bank robberies that had been committed by former Quantrill men.

Chapter Nine

Jesse James Gets a Price on His Head

Luke, Jenny and Kate stepped out of the Nimrod Long Banking Company and began strolling the boardwalks along the streets of Russellville.

"This kind of reminds me of a Western movie," remarked Luke.

"Me too," said Jenny.

"Indeed," replied Kate. "Outlaws like Frank and Jesse James, and lawmen like Wyatt Earp, have inspired generations of writers and film makers. And while some of their stories were pretty good, you have to remember that in the movies they're not always that interested in the real facts; they just want to tell a good story."

"Is that why, when we went back in time before, the things we saw about Wyatt Earp and Billy the Kid were so different than what was in the movies and TV shows we'd seen about them?" asked Luke.

"Yes," replied Kate. "Now there's nothing wrong with enjoying a movie or a show about the West as long as you remember that it's just a story. The real story of the real people is what you learn in school. And you know, sometimes the real stories can be a whole lot more interesting than what you see in the movies."

"We know," said Luke and Jenny together. Then all three started to laugh.

"We're now going to another Missouri town called Gallatin," said Kate.

Within the blink of an eye Luke and Jenny found themselves strolling a different boardwalk. The town looked much the same as the other towns they'd seen, but some time must have passed. Instead of trees that were ready to bloom they saw trees that had turned yellow and red with fall, and many had lost their leaves.

Kate turned them toward a building called The Daviess County Savings Bank. They stepped inside, but nothing seemed out of the ordinary. Kate told them to wait for a few moments. Soon a man entered the bank.

"May I help you?" asked the older gentleman who stood behind the counter.

"Yes," replied the customer as he reached into his pocket. "I would like for you to cash this one-hundred dollar bill for me."

Just then a second man entered the bank and joined the customer while the clerk began to write a receipt. The two men were talking to one another in hushed tones. Luke and Jenny couldn't make out what they were saying, but they could hear the name Major Cox and the word "sheets." Suddenly one of the men began shouting at the clerk.

"This is for my brother, Bloody Bill!"

The two men drew guns and fired at the clerk twice. He tumbled to the ground. Another customer tried to flee. As he ran for the door, the robbers fired on him too, hitting him on the arm, but he managed to escape. Once he got outside they could hear him yelling that the bank was being robbed. Luke and Jenny turned back to the robbers and watched as they emptied out the cash drawers and ran out the door. Kate told them to follow the robbers outside.

The townspeople, alerted to the robbers, began firing at them. Some of the bullets whizzed by Luke and Jenny as they stepped out on the street. Jenny screamed and covered her ears. She hated the sound of loud gunfire. They watched as the two robbers tried to escape, but the shooting spooked one of their horses. One of the robbers was trying to mount his horse and ended up being dragged several yards after his foot got caught in the stirrup.

"Look out!" shouted one of the robbers.

But before any of them could come to his rescue he somehow managed to free himself. He laid in the street for a brief moment to catch his breath as he watched his horse running away.

"Are you alright?" asked one of his fellow robbers who stopped long enough to let him get behind him on his horse.

"I think so," he replied. "Bet's get out of here before these good citizens form a lynch mob."

The rider in front spurred his horse and they sped away.

"They'll rob another man at gunpoint and take his horse," said Kate. "They'll head back to Clay County after that, and they'll manage to elude their captors."

"Who were the robbers?" asked Jenny.

"No one knows for certain, but it's a safe bet that one of them was Jim Anderson. He rode with Frank and Jesse James too and he was also Bloody Bill's brother. The bank clerk, the man they shot and killed, was a man by the name of John Sheets. During the Civil War he was an army captain who was involved in the ambush of Bloody Bill. Or they may have mistaken him for Major Cox, whose troops were also involved in the death of Bloody Bill. Either way, it looks like Jim Anderson killed the clerk as revenge for the killing of his brother."

Luke and Jenny talked about what they had seen

Bloody Bill do back in Centralia. They both agreed that he had gotten what he deserved. But they also had to admit that any man would want revenge if he thought his brother had been wrongly killed.

Kate went on to explain that the mare left behind by the robbers would soon be traced to the James Farm. It seemed that she belonged to Jesse, and the newspapers soon rushed to judgment by trying and convicting the James brothers for the crime in their pages. Jesse would respond by writing the first of what would be many letters to the editor of the *Kansas City Times* proclaiming his innocence and stating he had recently sold the mare. Kate mentioned that the editor of that particular newspaper, John Edwards, was an old friend of the James boys, with their friendship going back to their bushwhacker days in the Civil War. But many people would not buy his denials of wrongdoing.

"Meantime the people in Gallatin were so outraged at the killing of Captain Sheets that a reward of three thousand dollars was raised by the bank, the townspeople and Mrs. Sheets herself," said Kate. "And for the rest of their days as outlaws, Jesse James and his brother, Frank, would have a price on their heads."

Chapter Ten

A Raid on the James Farm

Luke, Jenny and Kate found themselves standing near a white farmhouse. Kate told them this was the James-Samuels farm that their mother would soon be taking them to visit and that the house was still standing. They watched as a small African-American boy came walking towards them. He was about the same height as Luke, and he appeared to be about Luke's age as well. As the boy approached Luke he stopped dead in his tracks. Luke looked the boy in the eye. The other boy appeared to be staring back at Luke with a puzzled look on his face.

"Can he see me?" asked Luke.

"No," replied Kate, "but I suppose he could be sensing your presence."

"Hey kid, I won't hurt you. My name's Luke. What's yours?"

Luke tried touching the other boy's shoulder, but his hand went right through him. The other boy did not respond, but he still appeared to be looking at Luke, as if he could really see him. The boy still had a puzzled look on his face. Luke tried speaking to him again, and again the boy did not respond. Luke kept staring at the boy, only turning away when he heard the sound of something rustling in the trees behind him.

"Look over there," said Kate, pointing to the wooded area around the farmhouse. A posse of men was approaching the farm and taking up positions behind the house. Two of the men rode up to the gate, dismounted and slowly walked towards the house.

"So *that's* what he was staring at," said Jenny. "I knew he wasn't seeing you, Luke."

Luke ignored his sister as he watched the two men coming closer. As they drew near the house the young boy suddenly bolted away and ran towards the stable. Luke took off running behind him.

"Hey kid! Wait for me!"

The little boy kept running.

"Mr. Frank! Mr. Jesse! Mr. Frank! Mr. Jesse!"

When the boy reached the barn door he flung it open. Out came two men on horseback. Kate identified them as Frank and Jesse James. They could see both brothers had their pistols in their hands.

"Let's give these boys a run for their money, Dingus!" shouted Frank as they spurred their horses to a gallop.

The posse opened fire and Frank and Jesse fired back as they raced away. The posse chased after them, but the James brothers had the advantage. They knew the lay of the land on their farm, and they were better able to steer their horses around any obstacles. Both their horses cleared the barn fence as they raced into the woods. The two men near the farmhouse door ran back to mount their horses and soon joined in the chase, but when they tried to take the fence after the James brothers one of their horses refused to jump. The other man's horse cleared the fence and he chased the James brothers on his own while the rest of the posse stopped to take down the fence rails. But by the time they finished it was too late. They knew by then that Frank and Jesse would have had too much of a head start. They soon left the farm, empty-handed.

"I guess that's just how it goes sometimes," said Jenny. "What happens now?"

"Now we wait," replied Kate.

A few minutes later the man whose horse cleared the fence returned on foot. Kate explained that after chasing the James boys through the woods he decided it would be easier to get a good shot at them if he dismounted his horse. Once he was on the ground he took aim and fired at the James brothers, but he missed. However, when he fired his gun his horse got spooked and bolted away and ran to the James' horses. Riderless, it chased after the James brothers until one of them shot and killed it.

"That's not right," said Luke. "That's cruelty to animals."

"Maybe," said Kate, "but the James boys had to do what they had to do. They didn't want the man who was chasing them to have another chance to fire at them."

They watched as the man came to the door and somehow convinced Mrs. Samuels to let him have a horse. Within minutes he was on his way.

"The James brothers will, as usual, get lots of attention in the newspapers," explained Kate. "And Jesse will once again maintain his innocence and say that he would be only willing to surrender if he could be guaranteed a fair trial."

"Were they really innocent?" asked Jenny. "After all, no one was ever really able to identify them in any of the robberies, right?"

"What do you think?" replied Kate. "Just because someone is handsome and charming doesn't mean they're innocent."

She went on to say that for years to come many more banks would be robbed, and in many, if not most, of these robberies the James brothers, their friend Cole Younger and his brothers, as well as other members of their gang, would be involved.

"It would always be the same," she said, "just like all the robberies we've already seen. They would come into the bank, take everyone by complete surprise and shoot the place up, oftentimes with innocent bystanders being hurt or killed. And then they would walk away with bags full of money." She paused for a moment. "Although there was one particular incident along the way that was rather odd."

Chapter Eleven

The Kansas City Fair

The James Farm suddenly faded away. Luke and Jenny found themselves among a large crowd of people. As they got their bearings they realized they were standing in a long line of people lined up at a ticket booth waiting to buy tickets. The ticket booth itself was only a few yards away.

"Where are we?" asked Jenny.

"We're at the Kansas City Exposition. It's a fair."

"Sweet!" shouted Luke. "Can we go in and look around? Can we go on any of the rides?"

"No, Luke, I'm afraid not," replied Kate.

Luke stomped his foot on the ground and began to pout.

"Lucas Edward Bartlett, you'd better stop your misbehaving or else!"

Luke looked at his sister.

"How come she knows—"

Luke was suddenly interrupted by the sound of three horsemen riding up to the booth. One man got off his horse, walked up to the ticket booth, reached in and grabbed the cash box away from the ticket taker. He quickly stuffed the money into a bag he had tied around his waist. Seconds later he threw the empty box on the ground and was trying to get back on his horse when the ticket taker came running out of the booth. The ticket taker started struggling with the robber but immediately backed off when one of the other men, still on his horse, pulled his pistol and took a shot at him. The ticket taker was unhurt, but as soon as the shot rang out they heard the high-pitched sound of someone shrieking. The crowd began to gather around a little girl who had been hit in the leg by the bullet. Jenny looked back for a moment and watched as the robbers raced away.

"Is she going to be alright?" she asked Kate.

"Yes, I believe so," replied Kate. "The James and Younger brothers will eventually be identified as the robbers, but I'm not so sure it was any of them this time. I doubt that Jesse would have ever attempted such a brazen robbery in front of so many people who would have recognized him. Especially since he's been pleading his innocence so much in the papers."

"So, we're not going into the fair, are we?" asked Luke.

"Sorry, not this time. But as long as we're in Kansas City let's go take a walk."

She led the two youngsters away from the crowd. Soon they were strolling the city's streets.

"It sure looks different," said Luke as he took in his surroundings. "We drove through Kansas City the other day on the way to Great Grandma Katie's farm. There were freeways and skyscrapers and lots of modern buildings and it didn't look anything like this."

"Well, Luke, you have to understand that places have to change over time," said Kate.

They strolled a few minutes longer until Kate stopped in front of one of the buildings. The words "Kansas City

Times" were painted on the front window.

"This is what I wanted to show you."

She pointed through the window at a man seated behind a large wooden desk. He was busy typing away on a manual typewriter.

"That's John Edwards."

"John Edwards?" said Jenny. "Isn't he that psychic on TV who says he can talk to dead people?"

Kate started to laugh.

"What's so funny?"

"You are, Jenny," replied Kate. "I'm not exactly sure who that John Edwards is, but some people do have that ability. In fact you and your brother have been talking to quite a few dead people for sometime now. Now you have to admit that that's pretty ironic."

"I hadn't thought of that," replied Jenny.

"This particular John Edwards was once Major John Newman Edwards of the Confederate army. He worked as a printer for a newspaper before the Civil War, and afterwards he became a newspaper editor. The day will come when he'll be hailed as one of the greatest newspapermen in Missouri. During the war he felt a great deal of admiration for the guerrillas and militiamen. That's probably why he became one of the staunchest defenders of Jesse James. It was his papers that would publish Jesse's letters of innocence, and Edwards himself would write many columns defending the James brothers as well. I'm sure he must be working on one right now as we speak."

As they watched Mr. Edwards busily working at his typewriter Kate went on to explain that although the James brothers would remain wanted men in Missouri for many years to come they would remain free to roam about, thanks to their family and friends and Confederate supporters like John Edwards. They would continue to rob more and more banks, and before long they would take on another kind of banditry—train robbery.

Chapter Twelve

The James-Younger Gang Robs a Train

Within the blink of an eye Kate had taken the two youngsters out of Kansas City and into the woods. It was a winter day and the snow was gleaming in the late afternoon sunlight. It was a stark contrast to the deserts of Arizona. Kate pointed to the small railroad station a few yards away.

"The iron horse, as some folks call it, is really changing the face of the West," she said. "It means more people will be coming here because traveling by train is so much faster and more comfortable than traveling by stagecoaches or covered wagons."

"I know," added Jenny. "When we were back in time in Tombstone the Swamper took us on a train from a place called Contention to Tucson. It was really cool."

"Yeah," said Luke. "And I remember one Sunday, before Dad got shipped to Iraq, we were hanging out at home and watching an old Western on TV about these two guys who lived on a train. I think they were secret agents or something because the train had all sorts of secret hidden compartments and other stuff. It was really cool too."

"I doubt if many trains actually have any secret hidden

compartments," replied Kate. "But they do have express cars that carry the mail as well as gold and silver and cash. And because trains carry large amounts of gold and cash from eastern banks across the country I'm sure it would be no surprise to you that the James and Younger brothers found them to be 'really cool' too. In fact, they found trains irresistible—for robbing. Especially when considering that the railroads were backed by the same Union bankers and businesses who wanted to drive pro-Confederate farmers out of Missouri."

As the three began walking towards the small station Kate went on to explain that the gang's first attempt at robbing a train didn't go exactly as planned.

"It happened in a little town in Iowa," she said. "Two members of the gang pulled up the railroad spikes and jerked a piece of one of the tracks away. They thought it would stop the train, and then once it stopped they would rob it, but things went terribly wrong."

"What happened?" asked Jenny.

"The locomotive reached the disconnected track and kept going. Trains are very heavy, you know, and they just can't stop that fast. And since this was the first time a train had ever been robbed west of the Mississippi they really didn't have a guidebook to follow. The engine ended up plunging into a ditch and rolling over on its side. The train engineer was killed and the fireman was seriously hurt."

"The fireman?" asked Luke.

"The fireman burns the coal or the wood to heat the water in the boilers that generates the steam that powers the engine. It can be dangerous work, because if something goes wrong with the boilers they can explode."

"Whoa!" muttered Luke.

"But luckily for the passengers the rest of the cars stayed on the tracks so no one else was hurt. But as soon as the engine was derailed a couple of the gang members ran into the express car."

Kate went on to say that an agent or guard always rides in the express car, but no one else is allowed in. And when the gang members forced the guard to open the safe they discovered the gold shipment they thought was onboard that particular train wasn't there.

"That's disappointing," said Jenny.

"Yes," agreed Kate. "And it's never good when train robbers get disappointed. In this case it seems the gold shipment had been delayed for some reason. So, not knowing what else to do, they decided to vent their frustrations by robbing all the passengers instead."

"As if they weren't upset enough by the train being wrecked," said Jenny. "That's cold."

"I agree," said Kate. "The James and Younger brothers were becoming more and more hardened criminals. And this time it was Cole Younger who wrote a letter to the editor of the local paper. He admitted he and his brother John were in the area at the time the train had been robbed, but he claimed that they were there attending a church service and that other people at the church could provide an alibi for them."

As Kate was speaking the three approached the little railroad station. A sign identified it as Gad's Hill.

"But just because one robbery didn't go as planned it didn't mean they wouldn't want to try again. And since no train has ever been robbed in Missouri Jesse James and Cole Younger just can't resist the idea of all the fame and notoriety they would receive if they were to be the first to do it."

Just as they reached the building five men approached from the other side. Luke and Jenny recognized Frank and Jesse James. Another man with them looked familiar too; Kate identified him as Cole Younger. She thought the other two men with them were Cole's brothers, John and Bob. The five men entered the station as Luke, Jenny and Kate followed close behind. They found several men inside who were stunned into silence as the five strangers suddenly drew their guns.

"Do what we tell you and no one will get hurt."

One of the robbers held the men at gunpoint as his four buddies went back outside. Luke and Jenny watched the other men place a flag on the train signal.

"They're signaling the next train to stop and pick up passengers," explained Kate.

After several long, agonizing minutes for the men being held hostage they heard the sound of a train coming. Soon it came to a stop. Kate motioned for Luke and Jenny to step back outside.

The conductor stepped off the train and was instantly taken at gunpoint by one of the robbers. Kate and the youngsters followed the other three onto the train.

"Cool," said Luke. "It looks just like the train in that TV show."

With guns drawn the three robbers entered the express car.

"Put your hands up and keep them up," bellowed one of the robbers.

The guard was forced to open the safe and then watch helplessly with his hands in the air while the other two gunmen looted it. Luke and Jenny overheard them talking about how smoothly this robbery was going.

"They really sound pleased with themselves, don't they?" said Jenny.

Her brother nodded his head in response.

"Let's have some fun while we're here," said one of the robbers. The three left the express car and went into the passenger cars with their guns pointed at the ceiling. Luke, Jenny and Kate followed.

"Gentlemen, we would like to see your hands. Just hold them out for us and don't do anything funny."

As his friends went to look at the male passengers' hands he smiled and kept talking.

"We're not going to rob any of you who are hard-working men of the soil, and we can tell working hands. And I want to assure you ladies that we will not rob or harm any of you either."

"We have one here for you," shouted one of the robbers.

This passenger was obviously a man of means, and all three laughed as his money and jewelry were taken from him.

"What about this one? He's got me mighty suspicious. I got a funny feeling he's a Pinkerton guard."

"Take him away and strip search him."

"What's a Pinkerton guard?" asked Luke.

"They're private investigators who work for the Pinkerton Detective Agency," replied Kate. "Some of the eastern bankers have hired Pinkerton guards to hunt down the James brothers, and as you'll later find out, they can be quite ruthless. Just as ruthless as the James brothers and their gang can be."

Two other passengers were also taken off the train, forced to strip down to their underwear and robbed as they shivered in the cold January weather. But other than being made uncomfortable and embarrassed they were not harmed. Kate thought they might have even been railroad executives.

"One thing is certain," she explained, "this public humiliation will later have dire consequences for the James-Younger Gang."

As the robbers finished their deed they hopped off the train and mounted their horses. One of them rode up to the train engineer and handed him a note before they raced away. Kate explained that the note was a description of the robbery for the newspapers.

"The train will go to its next stop a few miles down the line, and once it gets there the robbery will be reported. And because the robbers have also stolen mail the Post

Office is now involved, and it would call on the Pinkerton Agency to capture the robbers."

"Did they get them?" asked Jenny.

"Well, Frank and Jesse went back home to Clay County where, as usual, their family and friends would give them good alibis. The three Younger brothers went home too. Then Cole and Bob decided they would take a holiday in Hot Springs, Arkansas. John took sick and made plans to join them later, but he never made it. Fate was about to catch up with John Younger."

Chapter Thirteen

The Death of John Younger

As the three stood by the empty railroad tracks and watched the setting sun Kate explained that the James and Younger brothers were still seen as heroes among their neighbors for fighting back against Northern banks and businesses. However, those banks and businesses were becoming increasingly unhappy over their mounting losses. So much so that they decided the time had come to take matters into their own hands.

"Many times the local sheriffs would raise posses and chase after the James boys and their gang when the banks were robbed," explained Kate. "But once the gang crossed state and county lines they were out of their jurisdictions. And with the support of their friends and neighbors back in Clay County it was nearly impossible for anyone to arrest them, much less put them on trial."

"You know, Kate, that's something that I just don't understand," said Jenny.

"What's that?"

"Well, before my dad went to Iraq, he'd always watch the 6 o'clock news as soon as he got home from work. And sometimes I'd come sit with him and we'd talk about what was happening on the news. And every now and then there'd be something about a bank robbery and the police were asking for help in catching the robber. And my dad always used to say that if I ever knew anything about someone committing a crime like that it was my civic duty to turn them in."

"Your father is right," agreed Kate.

"So what I don't understand is why people didn't turn in Frank and Jesse James. From what you've shown me so far I think they're a couple of thugs. They're not just robbing banks and trains, they're hurting and killing innocent bystanders too, and that's just not right."

"Yes, Jenny, you're also right," said Kate. "There were a lot of innocent victims who got caught in the crossfire, and yes, those who knew about their wrongdoings should have turned them in. But it's the time and place Frank and Jesse lived in. It's like I mentioned to you before. After the Civil War ended the Northern business interests came into Missouri and made life difficult, if not miserable, for the people who lived here. From their point of view Frank and Jesse James weren't thugs; they were heroes fighting back against those Northern interests by robbing their banks. To them Frank and Jesse were like Robin Hood."

"Yeah, but did they share their loot with the poor?" asked Luke.

Kate laughed.

"No, Luke, I don't think they did. But still, to lots of folks in Missouri, Frank and Jesse James were heroes nonetheless, and they weren't about to turn them in."

"But our parents always taught us that two wrongs don't make a right," replied Luke as Jenny nodded her head in agreement. "So why didn't they bring in the FBI? They could have brought them in."

Kate started laughing once again.

"What's so funny?"

"You are, Luke. The FBI didn't exist until 1908.

And since they weren't there yet these Northern interests enlisted the help of the Pinkerton Detective Agency. But the problem was they just didn't follow the rules the way that regular police do. They were scoundrels in their own right."

As Kate was speaking the railroad tracks faded away. Luke and Jenny suddenly found themselves inside someone's home. Three men were seated around a table enjoying a meal together. Two of the men were young; the other man was much older.

"Mmm, that smells mighty good," said Jenny.

"Yeah," agreed Luke. "Come to think of it I'm getting kind of hungry too."

"Remember, it's still the middle of the night in your time," Kate reminded him. "Before long you'll be back in your bed fast asleep. But don't worry. Your great grandmother has big plans for breakfast tomorrow morning."

"Who are they?" asked Jenny as she pointed to the two younger men. "They look really familiar and I know we've seen them before."

"That's two of the Younger brothers – John and Jim."

"Aha," said Jenny, nodding her head.

Kate told them the older man's name was Mr. Snuffer and that his sons were friends of the Younger brothers, who had stopped by for a visit. Their meal was abruptly interrupted by the sound of approaching horses.

"You two, get up to the attic, quickly," ordered Mr. Snuffer.

As the two young men grabbed their guns and scurried away there was a knock at the door. When the old man opened it he saw two men standing next to their horses. A third man, still on horseback, waited nearby. As he stepped out onto the front porch Luke, Jenny and Kate followed.

"Pardon me, sir," asked one of the men. "Would you by chance know where we can find the Widow Sims' home? My friends and I have come to buy some cattle, and we understand she may have several head for sale."

"Certainly," replied Mr. Snuffer.

He pointed the way towards Mrs. Sims' home and gave the men directions. They thanked him, mounted their horses and turned to leave. But as they began to ride away they went in the opposite direction.

"That's strange," said Jenny. "Why would they ask for directions and then go the other way?"

"Because they're not really cattle buyers," said Luke. "I saw the look on that one man's face. I could tell they were lying."

"That's right, Luke," said Kate. Those men aren't at all who they claim to be. They're really Pinkerton detectives."

The three followed Mr. Snuffer back into his house as John and Jim Younger came scrambling back down from the attic. They were having a similar conversation.

"I tell you those men are too well armed to be cattle buyers," said John. "And did you notice how nervous that one man looked? I think we should go after them."

"Don't be ridiculous, John," said his brother. "Now let's sit down and finish our meal. We don't need to go looking for any trouble. We can always take care of 'em later, if we have to."

"Oh, you do what you want," John curtly replied. "I'm going after them, even if I have to do it alone."

He picked up his hat and started to leave. Jim reluctantly decided to go with him. He stopped at the doorway and turned to Mr. Snuffer.

"I'm sorry, but we'll be back again in a few minutes. Hopefully the food won't get too cold while we're gone."

Luke, Jenny and Kate followed Jim out the door and watched him ride off with his brother.

"What happens now?" asked Luke.

Before anyone could respond the three found themselves walking down a quiet country lane just behind the three Pinkerton men. The two who had stopped to ask for directions rode side by side and they could overhear them discussing what they should do next. The third man was riding ahead of the other two. It wasn't long before they heard the sound of horses coming from behind. They looked back to see the two Younger brothers riding up. They turned back just in time to see the man who was riding in front quickly spur his horse and flee.

"Hold it!" shouted Jim, but the man kept riding.

Jim quickly took off after him, firing his gun and shooting the man's hat off his head. But the detective was not hit and kept riding. After a brief chase Jim decided to turn his horse around and join his brother in questioning the other two men.

"Drop your guns," ordered John.

The two detectives did as they were told and dropped their guns to the ground. Jim got off his horse and picked them up. His face lit up at the sight of one of the pistols. As he examined it Kate mentioned it was a very expensive gun that had been made in England, and she herself had never seen one quite like it before. Jim looked back at the detective who had dropped it.

"Why thank you, sir, for such a lovely present."

"All right! Who are you and where are you from?" demanded John.

"We're from Osceola," replied the detective. "We're just here looking around."

As the Younger brothers asked more questions Kate pointed out a couple of farmers who had been working the nearby fields. They had stopped what they were doing to watch the exchange. The brothers weren't getting the answers they wanted, so John drew his shotgun from his saddle scabbard and pointed it at the man's chest.

"Enough of this! I want to know if you and your friend are detectives."

"No, we're not detectives."

"Really?" asked Jim. "So if you're not detectives then

why are you so heavily armed?

"Because we have the right to be."

John moved his shotgun and pointed it at the other man.

"So what about you? Do you have anything else to say?"

"Oh no!" exclaimed Luke, pointing at the first man. "Dude! Dude! Look out! He's reaching for something underneath his coat."

While the Younger brothers were busy questioning the second man the first detective decided to make his move. He pulled a small pistol out from underneath his coat as Luke shouted out another warning.

"Dude! Look out! He's got a gun!"

Luke broke away from Kate and his sister and ran toward the Younger brothers.

"They can't hear you, Luke," reminded Kate.

The detective took quick aim and fired at John, hitting him in the neck. His horse, startled by the sudden noise, bolted forward. Luke jumped back but not far enough. The detective rode right through him. John was able to return fire and hit the detective in the shoulder and arm as he fled. Jim fired at him too but missed. As Luke ran back to Jenny and Kate the other detective tried to escape as well, but when he spurred his horse forward Jim fired again, and this time he didn't miss. The young detective fell from his horse.

Despite the fact that he was bleeding heavily from his neck John Younger was very angry. He spurred his horse forward and chased the man who'd shot him into a nearby grove of trees. Luck appeared to be on John's side as moments later the detective was suddenly knocked to the ground by a low-hanging tree branch.

"Whoa! I'll bet that smarted," said Luke.

They watched as John, now starting to sway in his saddle, fired a shot at the detective while he was still sprawled on the ground. He missed, so he fired a second shot, this time hitting the man in the chest. Satisfied, he turned his horse around and headed back to his brother, who was busy examining the body of the other man.

"John!" exclaimed Jim as he looked up in horror.

John's face was chalky and white and his shirt was soaked with blood. He looked at his brother for a brief moment as if he were trying to say something. Then he fell from his horse, landing on a nearby fence. Jim ran up to him, but it was too late. John Younger was already dead.

"I see you wanted to change history, Luke," said Kate, "but that you cannot do. For whatever reason, this was meant to happen."

"He looked so young," said Jenny.

"Yes, he was," said Kate. "He was only twenty-four years old."

They watched a grieving Jim Younger gather up his brother in his arms. Kate ushered the two youngsters aside, explaining that even though Jim couldn't see them he was still entitled to a little privacy. He held onto his dead brother for several minutes. It was his way of saying goodbye.

Jenny looked up at Kate. She noticed there were tears running down her cheeks.

"Kate, what's wrong?" she asked. "Did you know John Younger?"

"No," she replied. "It's just that it's very hard to lose a sibling. My brother Carl died at the age of twelve. He was thrown from his horse and somehow broke his neck. And for the rest of my earthly life I never fully got over it."

She paused for a moment and then smiled.

"Of course now it's all different," she said as she took her handkerchief from her little drawstring purse. "I get to see Carl whenever I want and we do spend a lot of time together. But back then it was very painful, and I understand completely what Jim is going through."

As she dabbed the tears from her face they turned

back to Jim Younger and watched as he slowly let go of his brother. Then he took John's gun and personal effects. He called to the two farmers watching nearby and asked them to take his horse back to Snuffer's farm and tell Mr. Snuffer what had happened. He then mounted John's horse and began to ride away. He turned back in his saddle for one last look.

"Please, take care of John," were his parting words.

Kate went on to explain that the man John Younger had shot was still alive but that he would later die of his wounds. And Bob and Cole Younger, who were still vacationing in Arkansas, would learn of their brother's death in the newspapers.

"There would be a war of words in the newspapers after this," explained Kate. "The local sheriffs in places like Clay County were accused of not doing their jobs and harboring criminals like the James-Younger Gang. So the Governor of Missouri went to the state assembly and demanded they provide the funds for him to hire secret agents to capture the outlaws. We haven't seen the last of the Pinkerton detectives, but for now we're going to take a short break from all this gun fighting. Jesse James is finally about to get married."

Chapter Fourteen

Jesse James Takes a Bride

Luke, Jenny and Kate suddenly found themselves on the street of another small town. Kate explained they were in the town of Kearny, Missouri. It was a lovely spring day and the smell of blossoms was in the air.

"If you'll look behind you you'll see the home of Zerelda Mimms' sister, Lucy, and her husband," explained Kate.

Luke and Jenny turned around to see a very pretty house behind them. Jenny remarked that it looked something like a picture postcard. People were coming to the door and gathering inside. Kate motioned for Luke and Jenny to follow them in.

"You remember that time right after the Civil War when Jesse was recovering from that gunshot wound?" asked Kate.

"Sure," said Jenny.

"Well, he's about to marry his cousin Zee, the girl who took care of him. They've been engaged for nine years now, so it's about time."

"That is a long time," agreed Jenny.

"That's even longer than I've been alive," added Luke.

"Still, I think it's kind of creepy for cousins to marry," said Jenny.

"Well, for what it's worth, Jenny, Zee's family really didn't approve of the match either," explained Kate. "It's not that they didn't love their nephew, it's that they just didn't want to see Zee marrying an outlaw. But Zee is twenty-eight years old now. This is a time when most girls get married when they are still teenagers. For Zee to be unmarried at this age makes her an old maid."

"Really?" said Jenny. "Well, my aunt Cassie is twenty-eight years old and she's getting married too. My mom and grandma talked about the wedding plans the whole time we were in Dallas, and no one's calling my aunt Cassie an old maid."

"That's because you live in a different time, Jenny," explained Kate. "From what I understand people live a lot longer in your time than they did in my time, so it makes sense they would marry at a later age. And most girls in your time go to college and have careers. In my time that was rare. Very few girls went to college back then. In fact, a lot of folks didn't even get to finish high school. And in my time most girls started families as soon as they got married. Those who didn't die in childbirth usually ended up having a lot of children."

"Were you ever married, Kate?" asked Luke.

"Indeed I was. However, when I was young my dream was to become a schoolteacher. But then I met Jack and that changed everything. In the end it was my sister who ended up becoming a schoolteacher, and she never married. I'll tell you more about it later, if we have the time."

As Kate was speaking Jesse came to the door and was greeted by his uncle, Billy James. Uncle Billy was also the Methodist minister who was going to perform the wedding ceremony, but he didn't seem to be very happy. The two men soon had words. It was clear that Uncle Billy didn't want his niece to marry Jesse. Jesse explained to his uncle that much of what was being said about him just wasn't true, and while it took some convincing on his part, he was eventually able to get his uncle to approve. The wedding would take place a few minutes later.

"And it's not just Jesse who's getting married," said Kate. "His brother Frank is soon going to be married too. About a month from now he's going to elope with a woman named Annie Reynolds Ralston. She comes from a very good family and even graduated from college. She too was a schoolteacher before she ran off and married Frank."

"Did her family approve?" asked Jenny.

"No, they sure didn't. That's probably why she and Frank eloped."

Kate went on to say that Cupid's arrow would also strike one of the Younger brothers as well. While on the way to Missouri to visit his brother's grave Bob Younger would meet a widow named Maggie, whom he fell in love with and would eventually marry.

"So now that they're all getting hitched does that mean their outlaw days are over?" asked Luke.

"Not by a long shot," said Kate.

"Do we have to stay and watch the wedding?" asked Luke, wrinkling his nose. "I'm just not into all this romance stuff."

"No. We can let Jesse and Zee celebrate their nuptials without us."

"Nuptials?" asked Luke.

"It's another word for a wedding, Luke," replied Jenny, rolling her eyes. But before she and Luke could get into an argument the room faded away.

Chapter Fifteen

The Pinkerton Raid

Luke, Jenny and Kate found themselves in a darkened room.

"Where are we now?" asked Jenny.

"We're in the kitchen at the James-Samuels farm," replied Kate. "It's the night of January 26, 1875. What happens here on this night will haunt this family for the rest of their lives."

As their eyes adjusted to the darkness they could make out the wood-paneled walls and a fireplace. It was a very quiet winter night.

"What time is it anyway?" asked Luke.

"I'm not exactly sure," replied Kate. "But it's sometime in the middle of the night. The family has retired for the evening."

They heard the sound of approaching horses and people talking outside. Jenny headed for the window to see who was there, but before she could reach it the glass suddenly broke. She watched as large pieces of glass passed through her hands and arms, but she wasn't hurt. But in the quiet kitchen the noise of the shattering glass sounded like thunder. Someone had tossed something inside the house and it had landed at Jenny's feet. It looked like a flaming rag or cotton ball.

"What's going on here?" she asked.

She stepped around the burning object and peered outside the window. In the moonlight she could make out several men on horseback gathered in the snowy fields next to the house.

"Are they trying to burn the house down or something? And who are they anyway?"

As the strange, flickering firelight filled the room Kate explained the men outside were Pinkerton detectives and they were after Frank and Jesse.

"Are they here?" asked Luke.

"Nope," replied Kate.

They heard the sound of footsteps scurrying behind them. It was Dr. Samuels. He quickly grabbed a broom and began sweeping the burning object into the fireplace as Zerelda and their young son, Archie, entered the kitchen.

Luke walked up to Archie Samuels. He was a young boy with dark wavy hair. He looked a little bit like his older half brother, Jesse James.

"Look, Jenny. I'll bet he's about our age. I wonder if he can see us."

Before anyone could reply another burning object was tossed through the window. Dr. Samuels swept it towards the fireplace too. Suddenly there was a loud explosion. Jenny screamed and covered her ears. As the smoke cleared they found themselves standing outside the house. As they got their bearings they saw the Pinkerton men racing away. Smoke was pouring out of the kitchen window, and they could hear the horrifying sounds of people shrieking inside the house.

"What happened?" asked Jenny.

"The Pinkerton men just bombed the house," replied Kate.

"What?" exclaimed Jenny, sounding astonished. "Are they out of their minds?"

"I'm not sure," replied Kate. "Maybe."

She went on to explain that Pinkerton detectives had come looking for Frank and Jesse, not realizing they weren't there. What they had managed to do instead was kill little nine-year-old Archie Samuels and leave his mother very seriously injured.

"Her right arm will have to be amputated at the elbow," explained Kate. "And believe me when I say there's going to be a huge public outcry over this."

She paused for a moment as if to collect her thoughts.

"I remember this so well. When this happened I was the same age as Archie Samuels. That was when I first started to take an interest in Frank and Jesse James. When I was young I thought they were good guys. As I got older I realized they really weren't, but that didn't happen until many years later. But I still remember feeling angry after the Pinkerton raid, and a little scared too. I remember thinking that if the Pinkerton men could kill Archie Samuels then they could kill me too, or my little sister and brothers."

She went on to say that a pistol with the initials P.G.G. printed on it, standing for Pinkerton Government Guard, would soon be found by the fence. A grand jury in Clay County would indict Allen Pinkerton and several of his agents for the murder of Archie Samuels, but the case would never go to trial. Amnesty bills for the James brothers would also be proposed in the Missouri state legislature, but they would fail to get the two-thirds majority they needed to pass.

"In the end it was vigilante justice that prevailed," said Kate. "About four months later Daniel Askew, who owned a neighboring farm, was found with a bullet in his head. He'd once hired one of the Pinkerton men who was involved with the bombing, so there was talk that he had prior knowledge of the plan to attack the James-

Samuels farm. Meantime Jesse and Zee decided to move to Nashville, thinking they would be safer there. By then Zee was expecting their first child."

She went on to say that Cole Younger would be taking another trip, this time to Cuba, while Bob Younger decided to keep a low profile on his farm with Maggie.

"So was that the end of their outlaw days?" asked Luke. "I know if someone threw a bomb in my mom's house and killed my little brother I'd call it quits."

"No," said Kate. "I guess some bad habits are just too hard to break."

Chapter Sixteen

Bob Younger Backs a Bad Idea

Kate led Luke and Jenny into the wooded area near the farmhouse. The trees had lost their leaves and had icicles hanging off their branches. Luke and Jenny were glad no one could see them and that they could not feel the cold of the snow or the January air. As they were walking Jenny began to yawn.

"Are you getting sleepy?" asked Kate.

"A little bit," replied Jenny. "I guess it's still the middle of night, at least in our time."

"Yes, it is," said Kate. "But you've only been awake for a few moments, at least by your time."

Kate went on to say that in the weeks and months that followed the Pinkerton raid on the James-Samuels farm there would be more robberies, but many would be copycat crimes. And whenever anyone pointed the finger at Frank or Jesse James there would be their usual denials of wrongdoing in the papers. As they were walking the woods began to fade away. Within moments they discovered themselves in a hotel lobby.

"This place looks like something out of a Western too," said Luke. "So where are we and why are we here?"

"We're in a hotel in Kansas City," explained Kate as she pointed out a young man approaching the hotel desk. "That's Bob Younger. He's come here to meet with Jesse."

Luke, Jenny and Kate followed Bob down the hall to one of the rooms. He knocked on the door. It opened very slowly.

"It's me, Jesse. Bob."

They followed Bob into the room. Bob and Jesse shook hands and sat down at a small table.

"So, I take it you wanted to talk to me about my idea for earning us some money, Bob?"

"Yep," replied Bob. "But only if the spoils from this robbery would be big enough for me. I really need to buy a bigger farm, Jesse. It's like I was telling you before. I'm ready to retire from being an outlaw. I want to settle down and have a family with Maggie and be an honest farmer too."

"Okay, Bob, I guess I can't fault you for that," said Jesse. "So here's the idea I've come up with. We're going to take a trip to Minnesota, and we're going to rob a bank up there."

"*What?*" exclaimed Bob. "Minnesota! Jesse, are you out of your mind? We don't know the lay of the land up there. How would we find our way around?"

"I've got it all worked out, Bob. Don't worry about it. You know Bill Chadwell, don't you?"

Bob nodded his head.

"Well, he was born in Minnesota. He knows his way around and he'll be our guide."

It was apparent that Bob wasn't keen on the idea of robbing a bank in Minnesota. The two men talked awhile longer, but Bob remained unsure.

"Look, Jesse, I still don't know about this. I'm going to have to write a letter to Cole and see what he thinks before I can agree to be a part of it."

"I understand, Bob," replied Jesse. "Tell you what,

let's talk more about it later. We'll have another meeting next week in Monagaw Springs. I'll even bring Clell Miller along."

As the two men shook hands Kate explained that Miller was a man who had been with the James-Younger Gang for sometime.

Within the blink of an eye the hotel room faded away. They found themselves just outside another town. One man was waiting on horseback underneath a tree. Within seconds another man rode up to meet him. Luke and Jenny recognized him as Bob Younger. The two brothers greeted, then Bob outlined Jesse's plan to Cole.

"Now why would Jesse James come to you with such a foolhardy plan?" demanded Cole. It was apparent that he was angry with his brother and with Jesse.

"I know why," he said, answering his own question. "He's trying to sneak around me in making the decisions for this gang. He knows I'd never go along with anything this dumb, so he goes to my inexperienced baby brother instead. Why I ought a—"

"Get off your high horse, Cole!" shouted Bob. "My position in this gang is just as important as yours. Just because I happen to be your youngest brother doesn't mean you can push me around. I'm not a little kid anymore, Cole. I can make my own choices for my life."

"Yeah, and I'll bet Jesse put you up to saying that too," said Cole with disgust. "So now it appears that the great Jesse James has more influence over my own brother than I do."

"Look, Cole, Jesse has this all worked out. Chadwell's going to be our guide and—"

"*Chadwell?* He's Jesse's friend, not ours. And how smart are we to depend on one man alone for safe passage? Minnesota's a long way from home, Bob. A lot of things can go wrong. You'd better think about that."

Bob tried to argue some more with his brother, but it

was no use. Cole thought it was a bad idea from the start and nothing Bob could say was going to make him change his mind.

"Look, Bob, would you at least wait a little while before you give Jesse an answer?"

"Why?"

"I'd rather not go into that just now. All I'm asking you to do is wait. You've waited this long to get back with him, haven't you?"

"Look, Cole, I don't care what you think! I can do this with or without you. I'm over twenty-one now, and I can do what I want!"

"Alright! Alright! I've heard enough already," said Cole. "I'll tell you what. I'll agree to meet with you and Jesse if you'll agree to one thing for me."

"What's that?"

"You agree to have Frank there too."

"Fine, Cole. You have a deal."

The two men parted, and Kate explained that as soon as Bob left Cole sent for his other brother, Jim, who was now living in California.

"The three Youngers would have a meeting with Frank and Jesse a few weeks later," explained Kate. "And it would be a very heated meeting. Jim was as furious with Jesse as Cole was for approaching Bob with such a risky scheme, but Bob wouldn't back down. Finally Cole decided to play his last card. He told Bob that if he decided to go to Minnesota then he and Jim would have to go along with him to protect him. Bob knew that Jim was happy with his new life in California, and Cole didn't think Bob would want to risk Jim's happiness."

"So what happened?" asked Luke. "Did Bob give up on the idea?"

"No," replied Kate. "Cole's idea backfired on him. Bob was stubborn—more stubborn than Cole had realized. Bob told them that he was going to stand up and make decisions for himself, even if it meant putting his brothers at risk."

"That's not right," said Luke. "Sometimes I get annoyed with my sister because she's so bossy, but—"

"I am not!" interrupted Jenny.

"You are too!"

Before they could get into a bigger argument Kate stepped in.

"I think what your brother is trying to tell you, Jenny, is that he would never try to force you into going along with something he wanted to do if you didn't think it was right. Is that it, Luke?"

"Yep," he replied, nodding his head.

"You know, Luke, if you had been Jim and Cole Younger's brother instead of Bob, things might have worked out a whole lot differently for them," said Kate.

She went on to say that now with the other two Younger brothers onboard the gang would have to find a way to come up with the funds they needed to make the trip all the way to Minnesota.

"So they did it their usual way. They robbed another train."

Chapter Seventeen

The Rocky Cut Train Robbery

"So where are we now?" asked Luke.

He'd suddenly found himself out in the middle of nowhere in the dark. It took a minute or two for his eyes to adjust to the darkness. He could make out treetops, so he knew he was somewhere out in the woods. He could also hear the sound of water flowing nearby.

"I'm not sure," replied his sister. "But I see some railroad tracks, and if you look over that way it looks like there's some sort of building going on."

"You're right, Jenny," said Kate. "This is the Lamine River, and the Missouri Railroad Company is building a bridge here. We're standing right next to a spot called Rocky Cut. The trains have to slow down almost to a crawl as they pass through this construction site. That makes them easy pickings for the James-Younger Gang."

Kate had hardly finished her sentence before they heard the sound of approaching footsteps.

"Over there, I see 'em," shouted one of the gang members.

Luke, Jenny and Kate barely had time to step away as

about seven or eight men came rushing by. They followed close behind and watched as the gang got into a scuffle with one of the bridge workers. The man never had a chance of defending himself. He was outnumbered and quickly overpowered by the gang.

"That's the night watchman," explained Kate. "His job is to guide the trains through the construction zone."

They watched as the gang tied the watchman up. Then one took his red lantern and patiently stood by the side of the tracks. Kate explained that the red lantern would signal the next train to stop. The gang didn't have to wait very long. They soon saw a flickering light off in the distance, followed by the unmistakable sound of a locomotive with its breaks squealing as it slowed down for the construction zone. It approached very slowly, eventually coming to a halt at the red lantern.

"Here's where the fun begins," said Luke.

He watched the gang draw their guns and rush onto the train, then he followed Jenny and Kate as they boarded. The gang wasted no time getting down to business.

"Do what we say and no one gets hurt!" shouted one of robbers over the screaming passengers.

He and a few of his cohorts held the passengers at gunpoint while the others ran to the express car. Kate explained that the gang would do very well on this heist. They would empty two safes and walk away with more than fifteen thousand dollars.

"Wow!" exclaimed Luke. "That's a lot of money."

"Especially back then," added Jenny. "You would think they could have all retired on that without having to go to Minnesota."

"You know," said Kate, "in hindsight, I'll bet they probably thought that too."

They heard the sound of someone shouting. They looked back at the passengers. The man who was doing all the shouting was a passenger who claimed to be a minister.

"I'm a man of the Lord," he exclaimed. "And I'm going to pray, right here and now, for Almighty God Himself to deliver us from this evil den of thieves! And I'm going to pray for their very souls too, that they will turn from their wicked ways and that they will accept God's grace and accept our Lord Jesus Christ as their personal savior."

Shouts of "Amen, brother" could be heard echoing around the car.

The preacher was soon leading the passengers in a loud and vocal prayer about the wages of greed and sin. The robbers seemed to be amused by it all. Soon the minister led them in singing the hymn *Shall We Gather at the River*. Everyone seemed in good spirits. Even the robbers guarding the passengers joined in and sang along as well. Kate explained that they never had any intention of harming any of the passengers. All they wanted was the money.

As they finished singing, the rest of the gang, with their moneybags filled, tipped their hats to the passengers and rushed off the train to the sound of the passengers singing *Onward Christian Soldiers*. Once the hymn was finished the passengers and crew tried to regain their composure. Luke, Jenny and Kate stepped off the train and watched as it slowly pulled away.

"As usual, a posse will be formed—"

"And, as usual, they'll get away," said Luke, completing her sentence.

"Well, almost," said Kate. "This time they'd brought along a man named Hobbs Kerry. And, as I sometimes hear people in your time say, Mr. Kerry wasn't the sharpest tool in the shed. After the robbery he didn't keep any secret to the fact that he had just come into a rather large sum of easy money. That soon aroused suspicion, and a warrant was put out for his arrest."

She went on to say that once the authorities picked up Mr. Kerry he was quick to confess and name others in the crime. He named Frank and Jesse James, Bob, Jim and Cole Younger and two other men, Bill Chadwell and Charlie Pitts, as all being involved."

After this train robbery there would be another Pinkerton raid. This time it would be at the Ralston farm, but unlike the raid at the James-Samuels farm, no one was hurt.

"The reason why they took an interest in this family was because the Ralstons' daughter, Annie, had married Frank James," explained Kate. "But the family hadn't seen Annie since she married Frank the year before. As I recall Frank paid a call on his father-in-law a few months before the raid, but the visit did not go well and Frank didn't stay very long. I also recall hearing that the family was away when the raid happened and the man inside their home at the time was a neighbor. And I highly doubt the Ralstons' neighbor would have had any information that the Pinkertons could have used."

She went on to say that as usual, Jesse denied any involvement in the robbery in the newspapers. But before another posse could go after them they were already on their way to Minnesota. It would turn out to be a journey they wished they'd never taken.

Chapter Eighteen

The Northfield, Minnesota, Bank Robbery

The railroad faded away and Luke and Jenny found themselves crossing an iron bridge and entering yet another quaint little town.

"Have either one of you ever had days when nothing seems to go right?" asked Kate.

"Sure," replied Jenny, "I've had days when my hair didn't look right, or I missed the school bus, or I lost my homework—"

"Yep," interrupted Luke. "Especially since Dad's been gone."

"I see. Well today, the seventh of September, 1876, the James-Younger Gang is about to have a very bad day. It's going to be a lot worse than being late to school or losing your homework. For some it will be one of the worst days of their entire lives. For others it will be their last day on earth."

As Luke and Jenny looked around nothing seemed to be out of the ordinary. It was a pleasant late summer afternoon and people were going about their daily business.

"Look, Jenny, over there."

Luke pointed to three men riding into town. All three were wearing white linen dusters, or overcoats. They calmly dismounted their horses, tied them to a hitching post and sat down on some empty wooden boxes by a street corner while they exchanged hellos with the townspeople as they passed by.

A couple minutes later two other men, wearing the same white dusters, rode into town from a different direction. After that, three more men in the same matching white dusters came into town, riding across the same iron bridge, and stopped in the middle of the town square.

"Was Wal-Mart having a sale on white overcoats?" asked Jenny.

"Wal-Mart?" muttered Kate to herself.

"These guys aren't being subtle at all," said Jenny. "I don't see anyone else wearing white coats, do you Luke?"

"Nope," said her brother. "They might as well be wearing a big neon sign that says, 'Hi there. We're the James Gang and we're here to rob your bank.'"

Kate burst out laughing at Luke's remark.

"You're right, Luke. The way they've dressed really makes them stand out. That was their first mistake."

She motioned them to follow her towards the bank. As they were walking they saw the three men seated at the street corner stand up and walk in the bank while the two men who came into town from the other direction also rode up to the bank. Both looked familiar, and they recognized one of the two as Cole Younger.

"I think you'd better close the door," said Cole to his partner as they dismounted.

The other man, whom Kate identified as Clell Miller, was a longtime member of the gang. He walked up to the bank door and closed it while Cole pretended to be busy adjusting the cinch on his saddle.

"About that neon sign, Luke," said Kate, "you're right, they may as well have carried one, but neon signs haven't been invented yet. They're being about as subtle as bulls in a china shop, and they're arousing a lot of suspicion. That was their next mistake."

One of the local townsmen decided to take a closer look. He walked up and glanced in the bank window, but before he could alert anyone Clell Miller, who had just closed the bank door, grabbed him by the collar.

"Don't you say a word," he growled.

The two scuffled for a moment, then the man broke free and took off running.

"Get your guns! Get your guns! These men are trying to rob the bank!"

Cole Younger jumped back on his horse and fired his pistol into the air. Seconds later came the sound of gunfire from inside the bank. The three horsemen who had been waiting in the town square jumped into action. They pulled their guns and started firing and yelling at all the locals.

"This is not good," said Luke.

"No, and it's about to backfire on the gang," said Kate. "This time the locals are going to fight back."

She pointed to Clell Miller who was trying to get back on his horse. Just as he put his boot in the stirrup shots rang out and he was hit in the face. He fell backward onto the ground. Seconds later one of the gang's horses, still tied to the hitching post in front of the bank, was hit in the neck. It fell to the ground, dead.

"That's cruelty to animals," said Jenny.

"Maybe so," replied Kate. "But there's a lot of crossfire. It may have been an accident."

Four of the gang members rode back and forth, taking potshots at the locals. But instead of running, the locals stood their ground and fought back with everything they had; pistols, rifles, old flintlock guns – some were even resorting to throwing rocks. Some of the townsmen were shooting on the street. Others were taking aim from the windows of nearby buildings.

"It's like a war zone out here!" shouted Jenny as she covered her ears.

As the bullets whizzed by Kate pointed back to Clell Miller, who, despite his bleeding face, had managed to get back on his horse and draw his gun. As he turned his horse to ride up the street he was shot again. He fell from his horse as Cole raced up to him. Cole got off his horse and turned his friend over only to see the cold blank stare of death on his face. While he was leaning over his friend a bullet hit him in the left hip.

"I'll bet that smarted," said Luke.

Cole Younger ignored the pain as best he could while he reached for Miller's two pistols. And with more bullets whizzing by and an injured hip he somehow managed to get back on his horse and ride back to the bank door.

"Come out! Come out!"

He shouted desperately to his friends inside. But it appeared that his pleas were being ignored.

"Look over there, Luke," said Jenny.

She was pointing to a man who had suddenly come running from behind the bank.

"That's one of the bank tellers," explained Kate.

The teller was being chased by one of the armed outlaws. He fired at the teller, hitting him in the shoulder, but the bank teller still managed to escape.

In the meantime Cole Younger was still desperately shouting for the others to come out of the bank. They watched as another of the outlaws was gunned down by another local. As he toppled from his horse Kate told them it was none other than Bill Chadwell.

"Remember, he's the one from Minnesota—the man whom the gang depends on to lead them back to Missouri."

"Is he dead"? asked Luke.

"Uh-huh," said Kate.

"Then I guess they're gonna be outta luck," he replied.

"Come out!" shouted Cole from the doorway of the bank. "Please come out! We can't last much longer! We're being shot to bits!"

Kate rushed Luke and Jenny to the doorway of the bank so they could have a look inside. They heard the sounds of all the bullets streaking by and were happy they couldn't be hurt by any of them. They waited at the doorway until Bob Younger and Jesse James finally came out of the bank. Jesse stopped to scoop some money off the bank counter on his way out. Then they watched in horror as Frank James, the last man to leave, suddenly stopped, climbed onto a counter and shot an already seriously injured bank employee in the head.

"Geez!" exclaimed Luke. "What'd he have to do that for?"

"I'm not certain," replied Kate. "Frank was probably reacting to what was happening outside the bank. I guess he figured that if he wasn't going to get out alive then he'd take some of them with him."

They stepped out of the doorway to see the shocked look on Bob Younger's face once he saw his horse was dead. He quickly scanned the street and tried to capture one of his dead partners' horses. But the hail of gunfire made the task too difficult. With no immediate means of escape he was forced hide under a flight of stairs and play a deadly game of hide and seek with one of the townsmen. As he was shooting through the stairway openings Luke remarked once again that the scene looked like something out of a Western movie.

Suddenly Bob screamed out in pain. A bullet had hit him in the right arm, breaking it at the elbow. But rather than surrender he switched his gun to his left hand and kept fighting as best he could.

Cole decided he'd better do something to rescue his baby brother. He rode towards him, but before he could reach Bob a bullet severed one of his horse's reins. Yet somehow he managed to guide the animal close enough to Bob for him to get on behind him. As he turned his horse for his brother to climb on board more shots rang out. This time Cole was hit in his side and shoulder. Another bullet shot his hat off while another knocked off part of the back of his saddle. Somehow, despite all the gunfire and his broken arm, Bob managed to get on behind his brother.

"You know, I never cease to be amazed by the human will to survive," said Kate.

In the meantime Frank and Jesse James had managed to get back on their horses. It looked like they took a few bullets too, but in all the confusion it was too hard to tell. Kate pointed out Jim Younger, who was waiting for his brothers at the iron bridge. He appeared to be bleeding from a shoulder wound. The remaining bandits let out a weak rebel yell as they raced out of town, with a handful of locals chasing after them. As they rode off the gunfire began to cease and the gun smoke began to clear.

Kate looked down at Luke and Jenny. They both looked a little stunned at all they had just seen.

"It's not over yet," she said. "Now begins the long, painful ride home."

Chapter Nineteen

A Painful Journey Begins

Kate led Luke and Jenny back to the town square. They were still speechless. As the last of the gun smoke cleared, the town of Northfield faded away and they found themselves at a riverbank. Kate pointed out the robbers, who were in the river cleaning their wounds.

"We've lost Clell, and we've lost Chadwell," said one of the men.

"And our only route home," grumbled another man. "Did any of you think to draw a copy of his map? No! I told you all this was a bad idea, but would any of you listen?"

"Hmm," said Jenny, finally finding her voice. "That must be Cole Younger talking."

"Yes, and they should have heeded Cole's warning," agreed Kate. "I know how impatient you young people can sometimes be, but there really is something to be said for experience and listening to your elders."

"Uh-oh," said Luke.

He was pointing at a man approaching the riverbank. The man had a team of two gray horses hitched to a small

96

cart loaded with railroad ties. The man had no idea who the others were. He greeted them as if they were ordinary folks just passing through. His greeting was returned with the point of a gun. The gang demanded one of the gray horses and the man quickly handed one over. The gang took the horse and left, leaving the man unhurt.

"The people in Northfield have been sending out telegrams about the robbery," explained Kate. "But there hasn't been enough time to warn everyone."

She went on to say that they were going to follow the gang on their journey.

"But how?" asked Luke. "We don't have any horses."

"Look over there," replied Kate.

She pointed to a bay horse hitched to a buckboard wagon. Only it looked different. The horse had the same eerie glow that Kate had. Kate boarded the wagon and took the reins.

"Better climb aboard," she said.

"Where did this wagon come from?" asked Jenny.

"It was my father's," replied Kate. "Mama used to use it when we had to go into town, and we all rode in it to church on Sundays."

"What's your horse's name, Kate?" asked Jenny.

"Wilber. He was my father's favorite gelding."

Luke was fascinated by the wagon. As his sister climbed on board he stopped to look at it more closely.

"Luke, you stop your lollygagging and get on board right now!" ordered Kate. "We still have a few more things to see before you two can go back to sleep."

Luke boarded the wagon and Kate whipped the horse forward. She explained that there would be plenty of trouble ahead for the robbers on their long and painful journey home. She was right. As the gang entered the next town they could hear one of the locals shouting.

"Hey! What are you doing with Phil Empey's horse?"

The gang ignored the question and kept riding while

Kate explained Phil Empey was the name of the man they'd stolen the horse from.

Cole Younger was less than happy with the others, and he was not shy about letting them know.

"So how much did you all have to drink today? Could any of you have stayed sober long enough to get the job done?"

"You know I'm not much of a drinker, Cole," replied Jesse.

"Oh, really? So do you mean to tell me that you were actually able to come up with this nitwitted plan of yours while you were stone cold sober, Dingus?"

One of the locals jumped in.

"If you'd been riding with Custer and Sitting Bull was after you, you'd be riding a whole lot faster."

His remark was met with a pistol being pointed at him. The man quickly fled into a building.

"Custer's last battle at Little Bighorn happened this past June," explained Kate. "It's still big news."

The gang rode on through the town, stopping at a farm about a half a mile away. One of the men asked the farmer for a pail of water.

"What happened to him?" asked the farmer as he handed the bucket of water to Cole. It was apparent that Bob Younger was in very bad shape.

"He got shot by a blackleg in Northfield," replied one of the gang. "So we shot him and killed him."

"Who was that?" asked the farmer.

"A man by the name of Stiles."

As the gang began to ride away Kate explained that Stiles was Bill Chadwell's alias and that a blackleg was a gambler who cheated.

Jim and Cole were riding on either side of Bob, who needed his brothers to hold him up in his saddle. Cole's mood was unchanged.

"Jim?"

"Yes, Cole?"

"Did Mama ever drop Bob on his head when he was a baby?"

"I don't know, Cole. Why do you ask?"

"Because I still can't figure out how we could possibly have a baby brother dumb enough to go along with such a stupid idea as this. Mama must have dropped him on his head."

"Yeah, Cole," replied Jim. "And how stupid were we to go along with him?"

Luke and Jenny couldn't help snickering.

They soon crossed paths with another farmer in a horse-drawn wagon.

"Is that man your prisoner?" he asked.

"Yes," replied one of the gang.

"He's on his way to jail," added another.

"Well you're heading the wrong way!" exclaimed the farmer.

"No we're not! We're going the right way!"

Luke, Jenny and Kate followed along in the buckboard wagon. Along the way the gang stole another horse from one farmer and a saddle from someone else. But when the saddle broke Bob tumbled to the ground. They had to dismount to scoop him up and put him back on his horse.

They stopped in another town to water their horses. Kate thought that perhaps they were unaware of all the telegraphs that had been sent alerting the authorities about them and that a small posse had arrived ahead of them. Luckily for them the posse members had gone into the saloon and had left their guns outside. When one of them saw the gang watering their horses, he tried to come out, but the gang drew their weapons first.

"Uh-oh, here were go again," said Luke.

"Don't worry," said Kate, "no one gets hurt this time."

Unarmed, the posse could do nothing but wait until

the gang left town, which they soon did, with their guns blazing. The posse, now able to give chase, fired back. One gang member was thrown off his horse, and when he tried to get back on, the saddle cinch broke, toppling him to the ground. He jumped up behind Bob on his horse, which was still being led by Cole. They soon disappeared into the woods. Then it started to rain.

"It will rain heavily off and on for the next two weeks," said Kate.

"Strange," said Jenny. "We're sitting in the rain but we're not getting wet."

She looked up at Kate.

"I know. It's because we're not really here. Right?"

"Right," replied Kate.

She went on to explain that over the next few weeks a former Civil War general would be put in charge of capturing the robbers. The James-Younger Gang would be surrounded and forced to abandon their horses in order to escape on foot and they would hole up for a time in an abandoned farmhouse. But the ongoing heavy rains, while unpleasant, would give the robbers an advantage. All the mud and swollen creeks would help to cover their tracks.

"They were nothing if not resourceful," said Kate. "And they managed to slip through several dragnets along the way. But their luck would eventually run out."

She went on to say that as the reward for the robbers grew many men in Minnesota and Iowa came down with "reward fever" and joined in the manhunt. Finally the gang decided it would be best to split up. Frank and Jesse James stole a horse and headed west, while the three Youngers, with Charlie Pitts, another longtime member, headed southwest on foot.

"It will soon be the end of the line for the Younger brothers," said Kate.

Chapter Twenty

The Younger Brothers' Final Shoot-out

Kate and the two youngsters continued their journey through the lush Minnesota countryside. Luke and Jenny talked about how beautiful it was in spite of all the rain. Before long the rains stopped.

"It's been two weeks to the day since the Northfield robbery," explained Kate. "And it's been a long and difficult journey. Frank and Jesse will make it home, but it will be a different ending entirely for Cole Younger and his brothers."

As she was speaking she pointed out a very sorry looking group of men wearing torn, ragged clothes and limping through the woods. A moment later they disappeared into the trees and vines.

"It's time for me to send Wilber home, so let's get off the wagon."

"What about all this mud?" asked Jenny. "We're only wearing flip-flops."

Kate started to laugh.

"Never mind," said Jenny. "For a moment I forgot that we're not really here, so we won't get all muddy will we?"

Kate shook her head.

"Darn," said Luke, disappointed that he wouldn't get soaked with all the mud.

They jumped off the wagon and landed in the mud. Jenny watched with amazement as she lifted her feet off the muddy ground and found them perfectly clean. They turned back to the wagon and watched as it, along with Wilber, slowly faded away.

"Look, Jenny! There's a bunch of armed men coming our way."

"I see 'em, Luke. And look," she said, pointing in a different direction, "there's another bunch coming from over there too."

Kate explained that a very large group of men, possibly as many as one hundred, were surrounding the woods.

"They're all hungry for that reward money," explained Kate, "but, as the saying goes, and with no disrespect to you, Luke, we're about to separate the men from the boys."

Two men stepped forward. One was wearing a lawman's badge. Kate explained that he was a sheriff, and that he and the other posse leader were hardened Civil War veterans.

"From the North?" asked Luke.

"I believe so," replied Kate.

"Then that's not good for the Youngers," he replied.

"Listen up, men!" shouted the sheriff. "I need some volunteers to come forward and help go in there and flush out those desperados once and for all."

Out of the large band only a very few men stepped forward to help. Luke and Jenny counted only five.

"I guess this is what it means when people say you can talk the talk but not walk the walk," said Luke.

The five men were ordered to accompany the two leaders down to the slough, or muddy marsh, and spread out about fifteen feet apart from one another. They gripped their rifles firmly and carefully began their journey, watching everything around them. As Luke, Jenny and

Kate followed they heard the order that they were only to fire if fired upon, and even then to shoot low.

"Sounds like they want to try to take them alive," said Jenny.

"Yeah, but I don't think they'll surrender without a fight," said Luke. "They probably figure they'll get hung anyway, so what have they got to lose?"

Suddenly one of the outlaws popped up out of the brush and fired. The sheriff dropped to one knee and fired back, hitting the outlaw in the chest. As he fell, gunfire erupted from all sides as the many men who stayed behind opened fire as well. The Younger brothers, still holed up in the woods, fired back with all they had.

Jenny screamed and covered her ears and the bullets whizzed by.

"You're right, Luke. They're not going to give up!"

"Sounds like another war zone," shouted Luke. "And look, the posse's caught in the crossfire!"

Two of the posse members were hit, but their injuries were not serious. Stray bullets hit the trees, breaking off branches, which fell on top of the posse members. Jenny jumped back as a large piece of a tree suddenly landed at her feet. Gun smoke filled the air. It was as thick as fog, making it hard to see the posse as they hunkered down. One or two tried to fall back until the sheriff ordered them to hold the line.

Finally the gunfire stopped and the smoke began to clear. The other posse leader stood up. He checked his side, thinking he had been hit.

"What in tarnation?"

He pulled out a broken pipe, but there was no blood on his hand.

"Well I'll be. Look at that, boys. A bullet broke my pipe! Looks like it got stuck in my gun belt."

"Probably the only time in history that smoking ever saved someone's life," mused Jenny.

"I surrender," shouted a weak voice from the thicket. "Everyone's down but me."

"Hold your fire!" ordered the sheriff to the posse. "You! Come out with your hands up!"

"I can't, sir. My arm is broken."

"Then come out, slowly, and raise whatever you've got!"

The posse men looked down their rifle sites as some of the bushes began to move. A moment later Bob Younger came hobbling into the clear. His bloodstained clothing was torn and tattered, and he was covered with mud. He was waving a blood-soaked white handkerchief in his left hand. Without warning a shot was fired from the bluff above them. Bob was hit and fell to the muddy ground.

"I'm surrendering, you fools!" he shouted. "And you still shot me!"

The sheriff turned to the bluff behind them.

"I told you to hold your fire! I'll shoot the next one of you who fires a shot!"

A tense silence followed as all the men near the slough quickly reloaded their rifles. The sheriff and the other posse leader slowly and carefully moved forward through the thick brush. The other five volunteers followed at a safe distance behind. But when Luke and Jenny tried to go with them Kate told them to stay back.

"It's a very bad scene down there," she explained. "Trust me, you really don't want to see it, otherwise I'd never get you back to sleep."

"Are they all dead?" asked Jenny.

"Only Charlie Pitts," replied Kate. "He was another longtime member of the gang. But all three of the Youngers have managed to survive. They're a pretty tough lot."

They could hear the sound of people stirring in the thicket. Then they heard Cole Younger's voice, but it sounded much weaker than it had before.

"Come on," he challenged. "I'll take every one of you

on here and now! I can take any of you in a fair fight!"

"Chill out, dude," said Luke. "It's over."

"Some people really don't know when to give up, do they?" added Jenny.

It was as if Bob Younger had heard them.

"That's enough, Cole! It's time. Give it up right now or else they'll hang us."

"What difference does it make if they hang us today or tomorrow?"

They could hear the sound of rustling tree branches. A big lumber wagon was working its way down to the slough. Before long Cole Younger and his brothers were carefully loaded and taken away in the wagon. And while Kate didn't let Luke and Jenny get too close to the wagon they could see that all three of the brothers wore tattered clothing and all had serious injuries.

"So who are you?" asked one of the posse members as the wagon passed by.

"Do any of you gents have a chew?" replied Bob. "I really need something to help ease the pain."

Someone handed Bob a pinch of chewing tobacco. It would be the only response the posse would get.

"So what happens to Cole and Bob?" asked Luke. "Did they end up getting hung?"

"Well, that's what they expected to happen, but that's not how it turned out," said Kate.

Instead of being hanged, Kate explained that the Younger brothers were, in fact, treated very well by their captors. They awaited trial and recuperated from their wounds in a hotel instead of a jail, and many of the local ladies brought them food and helped nurse them back to health. And when the time came for them to go to trial they agreed to plead guilty, which meant they were all sentenced to life in prison instead of the gallows. But Bob Younger would die in prison in 1889.

"I think it may have had something to do with

complications from his wounds," said Kate. "He never regained the use of his broken arm, and he suffered from lung problems as a result of a chest wound. The cold damp air in the prison wasn't very good for him, and over time his body couldn't take it anymore and he died."

"So he never made it home to Maggie," said Jenny.

"No, he never did," replied Kate. "And I don't know whatever happened to her. She simply disappeared into history."

"He should have stayed on his farm in Missouri," added Luke. "Even if it was small, he still would have had a life and he would have never gotten hurt."

"You're so right, Luke," said Kate. "It's just like the Good Book says; you reap what you sow, and those who live by the sword die by the sword."

"Or as my Aunt Tina would say, they had bad karma," said Jenny. "So what about Jim and Cole?"

"They were both paroled from prison in 1901. But Jim would take his own life a short time later."

"Why?" asked Jenny. "He was out of prison. Wouldn't he have been happy to finally get his life back?"

"I can't be exactly sure why he did it, but I think it may have had something to do with the injuries he got during that final shoot-out. Jim was shot in the mouth that day and it did some serious and lasting damage to his jaw. For the rest of his days he was only able to eat through a straw. The bullet remained lodged near his ear and it caused him to have very, very painful headaches. He also suffered from melancholia. I think they call it depression in your time. I guess he just couldn't take the pain and suffering any longer."

"What about Cole?" asked Luke.

"You'll never believe it. Cole Younger would eventually be reunited with his old friend Frank James. And then he would go on to the lecture circuit. He traveled the country giving a series of patriotic speeches about the hard lessons he learned as an outlaw."

"Sounds like he was making a quick buck on his past," muttered Luke.

"Maybe," agreed Jenny. "But at least he wasn't robbing banks or trains anymore."

Kate went on to say that Cole Younger would die in 1916 at the ripe old age of 72, and at the time of his death he would still have 11 bullets in his body.

"Thus closes the final chapter on the Younger brothers," said Kate. "But even after this bungled robbery and the loss of their friends, Jesse James just can't stop being an outlaw. I guess some habits are just too hard to break."

Chapter Twenty-One

Hard Times for Jesse James

Kate led the two youngsters through the woods away from the shooting scene. The rains had stopped, the sky had cleared, and it was a beautiful late summer afternoon. They soon came upon a small pond. They stood for a moment and took in the beauty and the peacefulness. It helped to clear their heads and shake off all the tragedy they had just seen.

Kate picked up a stone and threw it across the pond. It skipped and bounced across the water.

"When I was a little girl my brothers and I used to have contests to see who could make their stones skip across a stream the most number of times. I usually won, although Carl was pretty good at it too. But Nancy, my little sister, couldn't get a stone to skip across the water if her life depended on it."

"How did you do that?" asked Luke.

"Here, it's easy," she said.

She picked up another stone and placed it in Luke's hand. He held it for a moment, turning it over and moving it around with his fingers.

"I didn't think I could touch or hold anything while

I'm back in time," he said. "Every time I try to reach for something or move something my hands always go right through it."

"That's because you were trying to do something that would have changed history," explained Kate. "You have a good heart, Luke, and you always try to do what's right and to help people. That's what you should always do. But you must realize that things happen the way they're meant to. Sometimes things may not seem fair and it can be hard for us to understand why, but everything really does happen for a reason. It's just that we don't always see it that way."

She took Luke's hand in hers.

"Now, let me show you how to throw a stone across the water and have it skip. It's all about throwing it at the right angle. There you go. Now throw it. Like this."

Kate held Luke's hand as he threw the stone. He laughed in delight as it skipped across the water.

"Sweet!" he exclaimed. "Can I do it again?"

Kate nodded. Luke had to take a few practice throws, but before long he was able to make his stones skip across the pond.

"That's cool!" exclaimed Jenny. "Can I try it too?"

Kate showed Jenny how to throw a stone, and within minutes she too was skipping stones across the water with her brother. Then she began to yawn, and Luke started yawning too.

"I guess I forgot it's still the middle of the night somewhere," she said. "All of a sudden I'm starting to feel sleepy."

"It's only been a minute or two by your time since I took you from your great grandmother's porch," said Kate. "But I still have a few more things to show you before I take you back to your beds."

She stepped away from the pond, found a tree stump and sat down. Luke and Jenny sat down on the ground beside her.

"Frank and Jesse managed to make it home from Minnesota," she said, "but they paid a very high price for the Northfield bank robbery. They lost some very good friends, especially the Younger brothers. And all they netted for it was a little over twenty-six dollars."

"You're kidding!" exclaimed Jenny. "After all that hassle that's all they got?"

Kate nodded her head. She went on to say that when Frank, Jesse and Bob Younger went inside the bank the employees did everything within their power to foil the robbers. They refused to hand over the money despite the robbers threatening them and shooting at them. And even though one of the bank clerks would end up paying with his life he still managed to keep the gang from getting anything out of the bank's vault. He told them there was a timed lock on the vault so he couldn't open it, and the three robbers bought his story. Had they actually bothered to test the door they would have found it was unlocked. In the end all they got was some loose money left sitting on the counter.

"So it was all for nothing," said Jenny.

"Yes," said Kate. "This time the old saying that crime doesn't pay really was true."

She explained that after Frank and Jesse returned from Minnesota they kept a very low profile. They soon left Missouri and moved to Tennessee with their wives. They may have even tried going straight, at least for a time. Jesse took the alias John Davis Howard and leased a small farm with Zee and their infant son. Frank and Annie, under the names Ben and Fannie Woodson, moved to another farm near Nashville, some ways away from Jesse and Zee's farm. The two brothers agreed it would be safer for them and their families to put some distance between them. Frank and Annie's only child, Franklin Robert James, was born on the farm in 1878.

For the next couple of years Jesse lived as Mr. Howard

a man too timid to take on a fight. But even with a new life and new name, things did not go well for Jesse or his family. In 1878 Zee gave birth to twin boys, but they both died within a few days of birth.

"That's sad," said Jenny. "What did they die of?"

"I'm not sure," replied Kate. "It could have been a number of things. You have to remember that during that time we didn't have all the medicines or vaccines you have in your time. It wasn't uncommon at all for families to lose children. I nearly lost a two-year-old child to pneumonia myself. Fortunately, my prayers were answered and he somehow survived, but my neighbors weren't so lucky. They lost their three-year-old daughter. That's just the way it was in my day."

She went on to say that Jesse's bad luck continued. During a hot and humid Tennessee summer he was bitten by a mosquito and caught malaria. He was very ill for a long time and unable to care for his family. In desperation he turned into an outlaw once again. This time he became a con man. He borrowed a large sum of money from a man named Mr. Johnson, but when he was unable to pay it back he bought a small herd of cattle from another farmer and paid for it with a bad check. He then sold the cattle under another alias so he could pay Mr. Johnson back. However, the other farmer never got his money, so "Mr. Howard" and his family had to abandon their farm and move in with Frank and his family.

While they were living with Frank and his family Zee gave birth to a daughter, Mary, in July of 1879, but Jesse was still having a hard time. Between bouts of malaria, being broke and having a family to support, Jesse was becoming desperate. He knew, however, that he had a career he could always fall back on. One that had brought him lots of excitement and money in the past. Only this time he would have to go it alone. His brother Frank had gone straight and no longer wanted to be an outlaw.

Chapter Twenty-Two

The Glendale Train Robbery

The lush Minnesota landscape slowly faded away. In its place would be an all too familiar scene. Luke, Jenny and Kate were standing inside of a general store in another little town. There were a handful of men standing around talking. They noticed it was getting dark outside, and they soon heard the sound of approaching horses. The horses stopped in front of the store. Seconds later several armed men burst inside.

"Do what we say and none of you gets hurt!" shouted one of the men.

"Here we go again," muttered Luke.

"Come with us, all of you," barked another robber.

Luke, Jenny and Kate followed the men and the robbers to a nearby train depot. Along the way Kate explained that Jesse had put together another gang. It included Ed Miller, whose brother Clell had been killed during the Minnesota bank robbery, along with several other men who'd served as guerillas during the war. Rounding out the group was Jesse's cousin, Wood Hite.

When they arrived at the depot they found the agent

already being held at gunpoint by another gang member. While the other hostages waited they watched as some of the gang members smashed and wrecked the telegraph equipment.

"You!" shouted one of the robbers to the railroad worker. "Go and change the train signal so the next train will stop."

"No! I won't do that," he tersely replied.

"What did you say?" hissed the robber.

He grabbed the agent by the neck and shoved a cocked revolver in the man's mouth.

"I'm going to give you one minute to reconsider. Then I'm going to ask you again, really nicely. Do you understand?"

A few minutes later Luke, Jenny and Kate followed the agent outside as he changed the train signal. Some of the other robbers began gathering rocks and piling them on the railroad tracks.

"This isn't like it was when Jesse worked with the Younger brothers," explained Kate. "Back then they had some compassion for the passengers. But this new gang is different. They're much more violent and they don't care if they cause a train wreck or not."

A short time later they heard the whistle and saw the flickering light of the approaching train. Thankfully it was able to come to a complete stop before hitting the pile of rocks on the track. The gang moved swiftly. They fired shots into the air from both sides of the train to scare the passengers. As two of the robbers jumped on board Kate pointed to the express car. The guard, carrying what must have been a bag of money, was trying to escape from the back of the car, but he wasn't quick enough. One of the robbers yanked the bag away from him while his partner hit him across the head with his revolver. Once the robbers were through plundering the express car they cleared the tracks and let the train and their hostages go. Within minutes they were riding away.

"Times have changed," explained Kate. "The newspapers are not going to be supporting the James brothers as much as they did in the past. Even their old friend John Edwards will wait a few weeks before coming to their defense."

She went on to say that after the robbery the gang split up and there would be rumors in the press that Jesse had been killed. But in reality Jesse and Ed Miller returned to Tennessee after the robbery. The two would even go into the horse racing business for a time, but it would prove to be unsuccessful. And after awhile Ed Miller mysteriously disappeared, never seen or heard from again. It would be rumored that Jesse had murdered him.

"Why would Jesse do that?" asked Luke. "I thought they were all friends."

"One of the Glendale train robbers got caught and confessed," explained Kate. "After that Jesse may have thought that Ed was going to turn himself in and name him as the gang leader. At least that was the rumor. I don't think they ever really solved the case of Ed Miller's disappearance. His body was never found and no one could ever prove that Jesse had anything to do with it. Still, I suspect there's a lot of truth behind the rumor. Jesse James could be a very violent man when he wanted to be."

She went on to say that Frank James, still under the alias Ben Woodson, had managed to remain a family man and good citizen in Nashville while Jesse and his new gang continued being outlaws. They were robbing banks, trains and even stagecoaches while traveling back and forth from Missouri and Tennessee. But times were becoming such that they worried old friends might try to betray them, especially after Ed Miller vanished and other gang members were captured. Frank and Jesse would often have to move their families around, at one point even taking them as far away as Alabama. In time, however, they decided to return home to Clay County, Missouri.

"It wasn't easy for either one of their families," explained Kate. "They were always moving around, having to go by different names, and the children weren't allowed to play with other children. Their parents couldn't take the chance of them accidentally squealing on them to their playmates."

"That's wrong," said Jenny. "Kids shouldn't have to pay for their parents' mistakes."

"Yeah," agreed Luke. "I'd really hate it if my parents wouldn't let me have any friends because of something they were doing."

"You two are very fortunate," said Kate. "You have very good parents, but not everyone is so lucky. And as for Frank and Jesse—their time is going to be running out. Very soon."

Chapter Twenty-Three

Frank Gets Back in the Game

"Welcome back, Buck. I knew your respectable life wouldn't last forever."

Luke and Jenny looked around. They had found themselves in the parlor of a modest but nicely furnished home. Kate explained that Jesse was now renting a house in Kansas City and posing as J.T. Jackson, a real sourpuss who wanted nothing to do with his neighbors. Jesse and his brother were having a meeting. Luke and Jenny both commented about how much older both the James brothers looked. Jesse had also grown a beard. Kate explained that the year was now 1881, and both men were now middle-aged.

"Look, Dingus, I was only kidding when I suggested you rob a government paymaster."

"All kidding aside, Buck, I thought it was a good idea. And I got about five thousand dollars out of that one."

"Maybe so, but it was way too close to where my family and I were living, and I'm still not happy about it. I've got a bad feeling it's going to come back and haunt me someday."

"You worry too much, Buck. But I didn't ask you to drop by so we could discuss old times. I've gotten word that none other than William Westfall is now a conductor for the Chicago, Rock Island and Pacific Railroad."

There was a long pause. Frank seemed stunned by Jesse's words.

"You mean the same William Westfall who was one of the Pinkerton detectives who bombed Mama's house and murdered little Archie?"

"The very same man, Buck."

"Well then, Dingus, I'd say it's payback time for Mr. Westfall."

As the two brothers began hatching their plans the room faded away. Moments later they found themselves onboard another train.

"I still think trains are cool," said Luke.

While he looked around, the train began to slow. Kate pointed out the conductor, Mr. Westfall, who, along with several of the male passengers, was smoking a cigar. Kate explained that they were in the smoking car.

"We're about to get in trouble again, aren't we?"

Kate nodded, and as the train came to a stop two robbers burst into the train car. Luke and Jenny recognized them as Frank and Jesse James.

"Hands up!" shouted one of the brothers.

The conductor did as he was told only to be shot in the back by Jesse. As he lay bleeding on the floor Jesse walked up to him and shot him a second time.

"That's cold," said Jenny.

"They're getting even with him for what he did to their mother and little brother," said Luke.

"Maybe so," said Jenny, "but it still doesn't make it right."

They heard the sound of a scuffle. One of the passengers was getting into an argument with the James brothers. He too was shot, but by Frank.

"Let's get out of here, Buck," said Jesse. "It looks like the rest of the boys are done in the express car."

Frank and Jesse hopped off the car. Luke, Jenny and Kate followed. As they watched the train pull away and the gang ride off Kate explained that when they divided up the loot the next morning they would all be very disappointed. Each robber's share only amounted to a little over one hundred dollars.

"Granted, that was still a decent sum of money, especially in my day," explained Kate, "but compared to some of their other heists over the years it was small potatoes."

She went on to say that the two brothers made their way back to their mother's farm for a short family reunion. It would be one of the last times that Jesse James would ever see his mother.

Chapter Twenty-Four

No Turning Back

"Times have changed," said Kate. "Even Mr. Crittenden, the governor of Missouri, has posted a five-thousand dollar reward each for the capture of Frank and Jesse James, as well as for the members of their gang. That's a very high price on all of their heads. The killing and the lawlessness has gone on for far too long."

Moments later they found themselves by another railroad track, although it was hard to tell in the darkness. The gang had just stopped another train with another pile of rocks placed across the tracks. Kate pointed out a young man who, with Jesse, was about to break into the express car.

"That's Charlie Ford," she explained. "He and his brother, Bob, met the James brothers through their cousin, Wood Hite. Dick Liddel, another gang member, has been courting Bob and Charlie's sister."

As she was speaking Jesse and Charlie managed to break through the door and rush into the express car. Luke, Jenny and Kate followed. Within minutes the guard had emptied the contents of the safe.

"Is that all the money you've got?" shouted one of the robbers.

"That's all I've got, I swear," replied the guard. "Take it, it's yours."

Luke and Jenny watched in horror as Jesse James and his young accomplice began beating the man with their rifle butts. Afterwards they ran into the passenger cars with Luke, Jenny and Kate following close behind.

"I'm Jesse James," he boldly announced to the frightened passengers. "And if any of you gets in my way I'll gun you down, right here and now. And I don't care if you're a lady or even a kid. If your screaming brat gets on my nerves I'll put a bullet in his useless little head."

"It's like the older he gets the meaner he gets," said Jenny. "What's up with that?"

Jesse then confronted the train engineer.

"I am not afraid of you and I'm not going to cooperate with you," was his response.

Jesse James calmly and coolly drew his gun and pointed it at the engineer's head.

"Then it looks like I just might have to kill you with the same gun that killed William Westfall."

Before anyone else could respond they heard the sound of another approaching train. The engineer of that train would have no way of seeing another train stopped on the track in time. The brakeman suddenly bolted away and raced down the tracks. A couple of the robbers gave chase and began firing at him.

"Do you really want to be hit by a freight train?" he shouted back.

"Maybe they would have had it coming if they did," commented Luke.

Fortunately for Jesse James and the others the brakeman was unhurt and able to warn the other train in enough time for it to safely stop.

Jesse James escorted the engineer off the train. As the

rest of the gang exited, Luke, Jenny and Kate followed. Jesse led the engineer to the front of the train and handed him two silver dollars.

"You, sir, are indeed a very brave man. Tomorrow morning I want you to use this to drink to the health of Jesse James. Now before we leave, would you like for us to help you remove the stones from the track?"

"No thank you, sir," replied the engineer. "I think we can manage just fine if you and your gang would kindly take your leave."

Jesse tipped his hat and stepped away. As the gang mounted their horses and raced into the darkness a voice cried out.

"Goodbye! This is the last time you'll ever see or hear of the James Gang."

"Public opinion is starting to turn away from the James Gang," explained Kate. "And the price on their heads keeps growing. They have become much too violent. And what people had once thought of as retaliation against Northern banking interests is now being seen as nothing but pure greed."

She went on to say that by the winter of 1881-1882 Jesse and his family were renting a small house in St. Joseph, Missouri, and they would be living under the names Tom and Josie Howard. Zee was becoming increasingly unhappy with her family being constantly uprooted and moved around. She begged Jesse to give up his outlaw ways. But even if he wanted to give it up, Jesse James just didn't know any other way of life.

Moments later the railroad tracks faded away and they found themselves in the kitchen of a small farmhouse. Several people, including a young woman, were seated around a table.

"I tell you I'm getting more and more worried all the time," said a handsome young man with dark curly hair and a mustache. "If Ed Miller could just 'disappear' then what about the rest of us. I tell you I'm done with Jesse James and his gang."

He pointed to young man seated across the table.

"Especially now, Wood, since your brother Clarence was fool enough to get himself arrested. How soon before he starts talking and gives all of us up?"

"Don't you go pointing the finger at me, Dick," he angrily replied.

"What about me, Wood?" asked another young man. "I'd be glad to take Dick Liddel's place. With Frank and Jesse being your cousins I know you could put in a good word for me. I'd be a real asset too, just like my brother Charlie here. Come on, Wood. Would you at least ask Jesse to give me a chance?"

"I don't know, Bob," replied Wood.

"Aw come on," he said, gesturing to the young woman at the table. "I'd appreciate it, and my sister here would appreciate it too, wouldn't you Martha? Tell Wood how much you'd appreciate your brother having a chance to be part of the James Gang."

"That's Bob Ford," explained Kate. "Remember me pointing out his brother, Charlie?"

Luke and Jenny nodded.

"Well Bob's been wanting in the gang for sometime now, but for whatever reason Jesse hasn't let him in, even though he's been friendly with his brother, Charlie, for sometime now."

As Kate was speaking they could hear the tone of the conversation around the kitchen table begin to change. The voices were becoming angry and loud. Bob Ford and Dick Liddel were having a confrontation with Wood Hite. Suddenly shots rang out and Wood Hite fell to the floor.

"What have you two idiots done?" shouted Charlie. "You've just murdered Frank and Jesse's cousin! What do you think Jesse James will do to the rest of us once he finds out? We're all gonna be dead men."

"They'll secretly bury Wood Hite," explained Kate. "But Dick Liddel knows there'll be a high price to pay for killing Frank and Jesse's cousin. So he decided the best way to survive was to secretly plan to turn himself in to the authorities and become an informant if they would agree not to prosecute him. There'll be no turning back now for the James Gang."

Chapter Twenty-Five
The Dirty Little Coward Who Shot Mr. Howard

Once again, Luke, Jenny and Kate found themselves at the James-Samuels farm. Jesse and his mother were standing in front of the farmhouse. Jesse was preparing to leave and they couldn't help but overhear their conversation.

"Ma, I really think you're right. Maybe your appeals to Governor Crittenden might have helped. Maybe if I do surrender and stand trial things will all work themselves out. But even if I do end up serving time at least Zee and the children could live here in peace. And if I'm not convicted then I can build my farm and live like a human being should."

"One more thing, son," said his mother. "I've had a bad feeling about Bob Ford ever since I met him. I can't seem to put my finger on it, but something keeps telling me he's not who he appears to be. Jesse, I want you to be really careful around him. Promise?"

"Sure, Ma."

Jesse reached down and scooped up a puppy.

"I can't wait to get home and see the look on my son's face when I give him this puppy."

He mounted his horse and tucked the puppy under his coat.

"Ma, if we don't meet again, we'll meet in heaven."

The three stood and watched as Jesse rode away from his mother's farm. Within minutes he disappeared into the woods and his mother stepped back into her house.

"More prophetic words could not have been spoken," said Kate.

"What do you mean?" asked Luke.

"Jesse would need to do one more robbery in order to come up with the funds to buy that farm in Nebraska," explained Kate.

Jenny rolled her eyes.

"Here we go again."

"Yes. Jesse was making plans to rob a bank in Platte City. He doesn't know it yet, but he's already been betrayed. He hasn't heard from either Dick Liddel or his cousin, Wood Hite, for sometime now and he suspects something has happened to them. This means he'll have to bring in both Ford brothers for this job."

She went on to say that Jesse and his family were renting a house in St. Joseph, Missouri, and that Bob and Charlie Ford were staying in his home while they made their plans. Unknown to anyone was the fact that Bob Ford had made a secret deal with James Craig, a police commissioner from Kansas City. If the Ford brothers could deliver Jesse James, dead or alive, they would collect a ten thousand dollar reward as well as immunity from prosecution.

The James-Samuels farm faded away. Luke and Jenny found themselves in the parlor, or living room, of a modest home. Kate told them they were in Jesse and Zee's home in St. Joseph. Moments later Jesse and the two young Ford brothers entered the room. Jesse, looking agitated, was carrying a folded newspaper in his hand.

"According to this newspaper Dick Liddel has surrendered. So how long have you two known about it?"

"Jesse, I swear, neither Bob nor I know anything about this. We're just as shocked as you are."

Both young men were expecting an argument, but none came. After a moment or two Jesse seemed to relax. He put the newspaper down, stretched and put his guns down. Kate mentioned that this was strange. By this time Jesse had become so fearful that he had gotten in the habit of wearing his guns around the clock.

Jesse looked around the room, and then something caught his eye. It was a sampler, hanging on the wall, which read, "God Bless Our Home."

"Hmm, I need to take care of that," he said.

He found a feather duster, moved a chair and stepped up on it. As he busied himself dusting and straightening the sampler he had his back turned to the Fords. And that was when Bob made his move.

"Dude! Look out! He's got a gun!"

No one could hear Luke's warning. Bob cocked his gun as Luke raced toward him. Jesse turned slightly at the sound of the cocking gun, but it was too late. Luke tried to grab the gun but his hand went through it, as if it wasn't there. Bob fired. The sound of his gun was like thunder. Jesse's head struck the wall as the bullet struck him, then he collapsed to the floor. Jesse James, at the age of thirty-five, was dead, having been killed by one of his own men.

Zee came rushing into the room at the sound of the gunfire. She screamed at the site of her husband lying dead on the floor. She ran towards him and cradled his head in her arms. Then she looked at the Ford brothers with a horrified look on her face. The Ford brothers said nothing and quickly ran out of the house.

"They'll wire Governor Crittenden and let him know the deed's been done," said Kate.

Within moments the neighbors, having heard the gunshot and the screams, came to "Josie's" aid, but it wasn't long before she slipped up and let them know her real identity.

"The authorities will confirm it's Jesse James by the missing fingertip and by the scars on his chest from the bullet wounds he received as a young man," said Kate. "By the time he's buried there will be no doubt in anyone's mind that the man Bob Ford killed was indeed the infamous Jesse James."

As more people came into the house Kate led the two youngsters outside. They strolled the streets of St. Joseph while she finished the story of Jesse James.

"After a funeral attended by hundreds of people Jesse was laid to rest at the James-Samuels farm," explained Kate.

She went on to say that Zee would file murder charges against the Fords. They were tried, convicted and sentenced to hang, but at the last minute Governor Crittenden intervened and granted both brothers full amnesty. They were free to go.

"Zee and the children would end up in poverty while the Fords would tour the country for a time doing theatrical performances about the killing of Jesse James."

"That's in poor taste," said Jenny.

"Maybe so, but in the end it caught up with them. A few years later Charlie would die by his own hand, probably in remorse for what he had done, and later on Bob would be gunned down himself. It just goes to prove what the Good Book says, 'He who lives by the sword dies by the sword.'"

"What about Frank James?" asked Luke.

"Frank was unable to attend his brother's funeral, but shortly afterwards he contacted his old friend, John Edwards, and Mr. Edwards arranged for Frank to surrender to Governor Crittenden personally. Frank faced trial for the Winston train robbery – the one in which he shot that passenger to death after Jesse had killed the conductor, William Westfall. But in the end Frank was acquitted."

"Why?" asked Jenny. "We saw all that he did. He was guilty more than once of robbery and murder."

"I know, Jenny, but it would take too long to explain all of it to you. There was some legal wrangling going on, and part of the problem too was the fact that Dick Liddel was not allowed to testify because he was a convicted felon. Then people's memories can get fuzzy over time and witnesses either move away or die. Knowing what Frank James did is one thing, being able to prove it beyond a reasonable doubt in a court of law is quite another."

She went on to say that Frank would face charges in Alabama as well, but again, due to some legal maneuvering, Frank James would walk away a free man. Eventually all charges against Frank James were either dropped, or he would be acquitted.

The three continued their stroll a few minutes longer. Finally Kate stopped. Luke and Jenny noticed that she looked a little sad.

"What is it?" asked Jenny.

"We've reached the end of our journey. The time has come for me to take you back to your great grandmother's back porch. You two have a big day ahead of you tomorrow. Your mother is taking you to the James Farm museum, which of course was once the James-Samuels farm. It's been well preserved. It's a lot like it was when Frank and Jesse lived there."

"What about you, Kate?" asked Jenny.

"I've got to get back to my family too."

"Can I ask you something, Kate?"

"Sure, Jenny. What is it?"

"You're not like the other spirit people we've met. The Swamper's still hanging around Tombstone because he's guarding his hidden treasure. And Paul can't get over the fact that he died very young and didn't get to do the things he wanted to do in life. But you're different. You don't seem to have any unfinished business. So why are you still here?"

"You're right, Jenny. I had a long life and a wonderful family. And I lived to be a very old lady."

"Then why do you look so young?" asked Luke.

"Well that's because we spirit people can appear just about any way we want. You're seeing me as I was on one of the happiest days of my life. It was the day I married my husband, Jack Ryan. We built a farm together, and we raised six children. And later on we had grandchildren. They're all with me now. All except one."

"Why's that?" asked Luke.

"Because I have one granddaughter who's still living. And every once in awhile I come back just to check on her and see how she is doing."

"So where's your wedding dress?" asked Jenny.

Kate laughed.

"Jenny, my family didn't have a lot of money. We couldn't afford a fancy white wedding gown. I got married in the same outfit I wore to church on Sundays. Now no more questions. I have to get you back."

Once again a strange streak of light flashed across the sky, and Luke and Jenny found themselves back on Great Grandmother Katie's back porch.

"It's time to take your shoes off and get back into bed," said Kate.

Luke and Jenny did as they were told. Kate stood by as they settled back into their sleeping bags.

"Will you sit with us for a little while?" asked Luke.

"Of course," replied Kate. "I'll just take a seat on the porch swing and I'll stay until you two get back to sleep."

As they settled into their sleeping bags Luke and Jenny could hear the creaking of the porch swing. Jenny glanced over and saw Kate sitting there. She had a look of contentment on her face. She looked back at her brother and a moment later glanced back at the porch swing. It was still moving, but Kate was no longer there.

"Luke?"

Luke did not respond. Jenny noticed that he had fallen back to sleep. She listened for a few minutes longer, and the porch swing kept moving, as if Kate were still sitting there. Finally she dozed off.

Chapter Twenty-Six

Breakfast at Great Grandma's House

They could hear the sound of a rooster crowing in the distance. Luke and Jenny stirred in their sleeping bags and slowly opened their eyes. It was early morning and the sun was barely up. They both yawned and stretched and sat up.

"Did you sleep okay, Jenny?"

"Uh-huh. How about you?"

"Yeah, but I had the weirdest dream."

"Really?" replied Jenny. "Me too. What was your dream about?"

"I dreamed this girl wearing old-time clothes woke us up and took us back to the days of Frank and Jesse James."

Jenny looked stunned.

"You're kidding, Luke! I had the exact same dream as you!"

Luke and Jenny looked at one another for a couple of moments. Then Jenny finally broke the silence.

"Wow. I guess Paul wasn't kidding when he told us we

131

have a gift."

She got up from her sleeping bag and went inside the house. Luke decided to take a seat on the porch swing. A few minutes later Jenny returned with a glass of milk in each hand.

"Here, Luke," she said as she handed one of the glasses to her brother.

She joined him on the porch swing. They decided it would be best to stay on the porch swing, drink their milk and compare notes about their "dream" before any of the grown-ups woke up.

"What's that?" asked Luke, pointing at the floor next to one of the chairs.

Jenny jumped off the porch swing. She went to investigate the spot where Luke was pointing and found the thick hardcover book that Aunt Vickie had been reading the day before. It was lying open on the floor next to the end table she had placed it on.

"Do you think that's what Kate accidentally knocked over last night?" asked Luke.

"Probably."

Jenny scanned the rest of the porch.

"I don't see anything else that's out of place, do you?"

Luke shook his head. Jenny closed the book and put it back on the end table where it belonged before returning to the porch swing. A short time later their mother came out to join them.

"Good morning, you two. How was your camp-out?"

"It was great, Mom," replied Luke. "Are we still going to start heading home today?"

Their mother nodded her head. She looked a little sad. Luke felt disappointed too, but then she reminded them their first stop on the way home was going to be the James Farm in Kearney, which meant Jenny would have more pictures to e-mail their dad in Iraq that evening.

"Mom, what's going to become of this place?" asked

Jenny. "It's been in our family for such a long time, but if Uncle Carl and Aunt Vickie are the last ones here then what happens after they're gone?"

"Yeah," said Luke. "Is there anyway we can inherit it?"

Ellen sighed and took a seat on the porch swing with her children.

"You know, that's a really good question, Luke. I honestly don't know what Uncle Carl plans to do with the place. It's really sad, I know, but the demise of the family farm has been going on since before I was born. Times have changed, and sometimes I wonder if it's for the better. I don't want to see this farm go out of our family either, but the fact is none of Uncle Carl's children want it. They've already come out and said they plan to sell the place once he and Aunt Vickie and Great Grandma Katie are gone."

Luke looked sad, but before he was able to start pouting his mother spoke up.

"You know, Luke, Uncle Carl also tells me that Aunt Grace's son, my cousin Earl, is very much interested in buying the farm from him. Earl and his son have decided they want to start up an alpaca farm and maybe breed horses too."

"Sweet!" exclaimed Luke. "Then someday we can come back to visit our cousins and ride the horses too!"

"I don't know about that, son. It's hardly a done deal. It's all up to your uncle Carl and aunt Vickie to decide. But right now I want you two to go inside and get dressed. Before we leave your great grandmother wants us all to have breakfast together in the dining room. It's going to be our last meal together and this is a very big deal for her. She even wants us to use the fine china that she only uses at Thanksgiving and Christmas."

After Luke and Jenny got dressed they went into the kitchen to help their mother and Aunt Vickie prepare breakfast. Aunt Vickie was making eggs benedict while their mother was busy chopping up cantaloupe, watermelon and strawberries for a fresh fruit salad.

"I need you guys to set the table," said their mother. "But please be very careful. Great Grandma Katie's fine china is over fifty years old."

Luke and Jenny carefully set the dining room table with Great Grandmother Katie's sterling silverware, fine china and crystal glassware. As they were finishing, their mother brought in a big bouquet of fresh cut flowers in a beautiful blue cut glass vase.

"These are from your aunt Vickie's flower garden," she said as she placed the bouquet in the center of the table. "Isn't it beautiful?"

"It sure is," agreed Jenny.

"And you two did a great job setting the table. This is going to be a very special meal indeed."

They came back into the kitchen with their mother. The phone began to ring and Uncle Carl grabbed the receiver.

"Angie! How are you?"

There was a brief moment of silence on his end.

"Yes, Angie, they're still here. They'll be leaving later on this morning."

There was another pause.

"Actually, it's been great having them here. Hey, I still have to tell the kids about the time you and Daniel dropped out of college and ran off to California to become hippies."

There was another brief pause as he laughed and handed the phone to Luke and Jenny's mother. While she was busy chatting on the phone with her mother Luke and Jenny turned to see Great Grandmother Katie standing outside the kitchen doorway. She was wearing a beautiful white dress with red roses printed on it.

"Good morning, Great Grandma," said Jenny. "You sure look pretty today."

"Thank you," she replied. "I wanted to look nice today. You and your mother probably won't get to see me again, so I wanted you all to have a special memory of me before you leave."

She stood quietly for a moment as she leaned on her cane and watched her family bustling about in the kitchen. Jenny noticed her eyes were welling up with tears.

"Are you okay, Great Grandma?" she asked.

"Yes, Jenny" she replied. "I was just having a moment. I was thinking about how blessed I've been to have had such a wonderful family."

"Luke!" called Aunt Vickie. "Would you and your sister mind escorting your great grandmother into the dining room and keeping her company there? Breakfast will be ready in a few minutes."

Luke extended his elbow to his great grandmother. She took his arm and let him lead her into the dining room. Jenny followed close behind and helped seat her at the head of the dining room table. While they waited for breakfast to arrive Luke and Jenny decided to have a closer look at all the family photos that hung on the walls. Some photos looked fairly recent. Others had faded colors, and many were in black and white. There were even a few old-time sepia tone portraits. The entire dining room was a big photo gallery of their family history.

Their great grandmother pointed out one of the photos. It was an old color picture of two young people wearing blue jeans and floral printed smocks standing in front of the Golden Gate Bridge. Both were wearing what looked like hand-beaded necklaces. The color in the photo had faded so much that it almost looked black and white. The two people in it both had long hair parted down the middle. One was a blonde woman who wore a pair of round wire-framed sunglasses. The man had what looked like reddish brown hair and a beard with a leather headband tied across his forehead.

"I overheard your great uncle on the phone with your grandmother," said Great Grandmother Katie. "That's your grandparents in their hippie days. That picture was taken in the summer of 1968, about a year before they got married. Angie was quite the rebel back then."

"Wow!" said Jenny. "They both looked so different back then. I hardly recognize Grandpa with the beard and all that long hair. But now that I look at it I think Grandma looks a lot the same. It's just that her hair's turned white now and she doesn't wear it as long anymore."

"She kind of looks like you, Jenny," added Luke.

"Yes, you do look a lot like your grandmother did when she was a young girl. So does your mother."

Luke and Jenny looked at more of the photos on the wall as their great grandmother explained to them who the different people were. One picture in particular caught Jenny's eye. It was an old black and white photo of two women standing next to an old car. One woman was young, and the other was elderly. They were both dressed in very nice dresses and both were wearing fancy hats and flower corsages. They were standing in front of the farmhouse, only the house looked different. It was smaller, and there was no second story.

"That's me, about a year after I married your great grandfather," explained Great Grandmother Katie. "It was Mother's Day and we were on our way to church. I was expecting your great uncle Carl when that picture was taken."

Luke and Jenny looked closer at the photo. They noticed their great grandmother had just a little bit of a tummy sticking out.

"It's a shame that picture wasn't in color. I had such beautiful red hair back then."

As they looked at the photo again they noticed something seemed familiar about the older woman standing next to their great grandmother.

"Who is that with you?" asked Jenny.

"Why that's my grandmother," explained Great

Grandmother Katie. "She and I were always very close and she used to visit me a lot. Your great grandfather was quite fond of her too. So when our son was born we decided to name him Carl after my grandmother's brother. He died at a young age and Grandmother never fully recovered from it."

Luke and Jenny looked at one another.

"What happened to him?" asked Jenny.

"The story goes that he was thrown from his horse and somehow broke his neck when he fell."

Luke and Jenny looked at each other again as they recalled Kate's story of a brother named Carl who had also suffered the same fate.

"You know," said Great Grandma Katie, "from time to time I get the feeling that my grandmother is still here with me, even now. It's almost like she's in the room with me, but don't go telling your mother that. You know how she is."

"We know," said Luke and Jenny together.

"Anyway, I was named after her. Her name was Kathleen. Kathleen Elizabeth Ryan, but everyone called her Kate. I was named Kathleen Suzanne, after my grandmother, and Jenny, you were named Jennifer Kathleen after me. It's kind of nice having her name passed down the family, don't you think?"

Luke and Jenny looked at one another with a knowing look in their eyes. They both looked back at the photo again just to be sure. Even though she was much older in the photo, they knew, without a doubt, that their great grandmother's grandmother was none other than Kate.

THE END

A Guide for Parents and Teachers

While the story of Luke and Jenny is fiction, their adventures with the James brothers are based on actual historical events. The following guide may be useful in developing lesson plans from this book to help your students learn more about the Civil War and the American West.

Guerrilla Warfare. The Civil War battles weren't just between armies; there were non-military militia groups fighting as well. Have your students research these groups. Were there any pro-Union militia groups? Who were their leaders? What types of things did these groups, both pro-Union and pro-Confederate, do to civilians?

William Tecumseh Sherman. Who was William Tecumseh Sherman? Have your students do some research to learn who he was, learn about his scorched earth policies and why some consider Sherman to be the first modern general.

The Post Civil War South. Who were the Carpetbaggers? Why were they so hated by the post-Civil War Southerners?

The Railroad and Westward Expansion. The railroad changed the face of the American West. Have your students do some research on the history of train travel and its role in westward expansion.

Steam Trains. Steam powered locomotives were the high-tech wonders of their day. Have your students research steam powered engines. How did they work? What kind of fuel did they use?

References

Bell, Bob Boze. *Classic Gunfights Volume One.* Phoenix, Arizona: Tri Star – Boze Publications, Inc. 2003.

Brant, Marely. *The Illustrated History of the James-Younger Gang.* Montgomery, Alabama: Elliot & Clark Publishing. 1997.

Nash, Jay Robert. *Encyclopedia of Western Lawmen & Outlaws.* New York: Da Capo Press. 1994.

On-line interviews with Milt Fairchild, local historian, Osceola, Missouri.

Settle, William A., Jr. *Jesse James Was His Name.* Lincoln, Nebraska: Bison Books and University of Nebraska Press. 1977.

Other Luke and Jenny historical adventures
by Gayle Martin

Gunfight at the O.K. Corral: Luke and Jenny Visit Tombstone

Billy the Kid and the Lincoln County War: a Luke and Jenny Adventure

For more information on Luke and Jenny and thier adventures in time please be sure to visit our website at LukeandJennyBooks.com.